PICNIC ON A CIRCUS TRAIN

PICNIC ON A CIRCUS TRAIN

a novel by

Charles Gillespie

Goldsmith / Kesheru
Dublin, New Hampshire

Published by Goldsmith / Kesheru, LLC
Post Office Box One Zero Six
Dublin, New Hampshire 03444

Printed in the United States of America

This book is a work of fiction.
The characters and events described are a product of the author's imagination.

Grateful acknowledgement is extended to the editors of the following periodicals,
wherein certain chapters have appeared in slightly different versions:
Western Humanities Review: Chapter 2 as "Jack Learns His Lesson"
Ball State University Press: Chapter 3 as "Barrel of Fun"
Descant: Chapter 4 as "Days Begin and Days End"
University of Portland Review: Chapter 5 as "A Roll Is Called"
Natural Bridge: Chapter 9 as "A Rest for The Weary"
Prairie Schooner: Chapter 10 as "Trees, But Rare Shade"

Lyrics from "Tie Me To Your Apron Strings Again,"
were written by Joe Goodwin and published by
Milton Weil Music Company, Inc., 1925.

ISBN-13: 978-0-9844934-0-1
ISBN-10: 0-9844934-0-9

Cover Art / C. Meng

0 8 6 4 2 1 3 5 7 9

for Addie Lee

Picnic on a Circus Train

1

WIND, almost the winter's wind, began early that day; becoming, by noon, so intense the miles around glittered with blowing sand. Gold dust some of it.

Sad men at work on the great canal turned away from the wind, digging backward, moving forward. Sad men damaged in well-known wars walked into the wind, eyes downcast, eyes near closed in the glitter; assuming an attitude of prayer to curse God and his curse on themselves. Jewels could be lost in the dust, and religion, and discoveries, and Jack Desbrough could be born in it, was born in it on the third day of March in 1933.

* * *

On the third day of March of 1940 the same wind hung visibly upon the county. Jack Desbrough was seven years old, wiser now to the probabilities of death than to the possibilities of birth, although much closer to the one than to the other.

For the first few years, Jack had no image of the unpleasant save that of a white Leghorn rooster chasing him around the horse trough while the two ragged cowboys who worked with his father on the ratty little ranch pleaded for him to turn on the clucking villain. He would have, if he could have.

Jack's mother ended the rooster's triumph, at last, by wringing its fowl neck during another bleak and cold morning. Bleak and cold, that is, for all except Jack, who watched the headless death dance from the porch of the unpainted little house, eating a buttered cracker and glowing at the spectacle of an enemy groveling in the dust, flinging clouds of dirt on its own feathers, scattering clots of blood about the barren back yard and the white caliche rocks that decorated it. Had it not been for the death of the rooster the morning would have otherwise been the kind Jack would frequently regret. The day was one of the coldest, a bare West Texas day with the bright sun frozen, though at least the wind was stilled.

With the rooster removed from memory, Jack's years were pleasantly lonely. The family was poor, but poverty is of vague consequence to the very young unless called to their attention by other young. Jack lacked both the boldness and the cruelty which might have made him a novelty to the cowboys. He was the only available grandson of the grandfather: a skinny, white-haired old man who did not especially like small children and who missed the history which, later, every other grandfather seemed to have been a part of though he would, sometimes, relate an array of anecdotes concerning ghosts and gold in the Davis Mountains, of men bitten by mad dogs and dying—years later—while shingling their roofs, and of great, cool caves in the desert filled with treasures smothered beneath the weight of hundreds of rattlesnakes, live ones coiled on the bones of dead ones, all of them rattling in their own way. It was this grandfather who told Jack how much God loved this windswept part of the world, leaving neither stone mountain nor living forest nor moving water to interrupt his view of the great plain.

One day the grandfather was gone, dead in the night. Not many days afterward he was also forgotten except in later years when the old face with the white hair would come to mind whenever the name of God or a similarly elusive presence was mentioned in Jack's hearing.

Jack's father had no ambitions recognizable as ambitions for himself, but when Jack's younger brother was born his father left the mesquite beans and the castrating, the smells of dry manure and dry earth, the horses and the barbed wire and the splintering barns that had always been his life and moved to Goldsmith, a town newly erupted from an oil boom at an unnatural crossing of ranch roads in an obscure corner of the prairie.

Asleep when the move was accomplished, Jack's first sight of the unpainted, flat little town came from the tautly-screened back door of his own new home. All he could see was a world of discarded lumber strewn and stacked in puzzling arrays. Not again did the town look like that, not even the next morning, so Jack could never be certain whether he had dreamed the scene or if it had actually been one day's wonder, never again to be repeated.

* * *

Jack sat, naked, in a large washtub in one cell of the small jail located behind his house. The washtub was new and shiny with a galvanized glamour as Jack himself was new and shiny. Even the jail, two square concrete rooms located between the outhouse and the corral, was new. Across the yard—weedless, crusted earth sprinkled with sand and white rocks—Jack could see into the kitchen door where his mother stood singing hymns, an assistance in the vigilance of seeing that Jack did not drown in a washtub full of bathwater, one of the ways of death he was constantly reminded to be aware of. Compiled in a loose-leaf,

5

expandable notebook, the warnings would comprise an incredible journal of peril, with dangers catalogued for instant reference: no screwing around with stray kittens, no chewing unidentifiable grass, no sipping bath water, no lingering behind placid cows, no drinking after another person unless the person was your brother. Jack considered urinating into the washtub, but his mother's sweet voice filtered through the rocks and the morning and he decided, in a gesture of fondness, that he would not. The words he could hear were of the Blessed Redeemer "Praying for Sinners while in Such Woe."

Woe seemed to be exactly what Jack was in, pursued by destruction in daylight; sought by a grisly, black and snaggle-toothed evil in the darkness. He was not afraid.

From the house next door, the new neighbor came into the yard carrying a bundle of damp clothing in a basket under her arm. She was a small woman, still pretty from her childhood, the childhood ended only recently by the responsibilities of teaching fifth-grade Texas history. She walked past Jack as he stood in the pool of water.

"Look at me," he shouted. "I'm a man." The woman did not look.

A few minutes later, the kitchen door opened and Jack's father strode outside, stripping the belt from his trousers as he walked. Jack knew he was about to experience an unpleasantness, but instead of fear he could only feel admiration for adult effectiveness, the swashbuckling manner of the belt's unscabbering, the silver buckle shining in the sunlight, the carved brown leather slicing through the loops of the trousers, faintly fluttering at the end and then dangling. Deadly in his father's large hand.

Jack's father used the belt swiftly, resolutely, not even pausing to speak angrily. Afterward, Jack cried furiously, more from his weakness at feeling pain that from the actual pain. When the

6

woman, returning to her house, glanced uneasily at him, Jack stopped crying and shouted at her.

"I'm not crying."

A grimness settled into his jaw as certainly as though a master in a London saloon had tattooed it there. "I'll never show anybody anything again," he thought.

Wiser now by far, Jack sat in the tub, washing his feet and then his face, polishing the concrete floor around the tub, listening—pleased—as his mother resumed singing. He had forgotten his father's anger; even his father.

The business of growing up had already become a tedium to Jack Desbrough. Within the next two years he would occasionally doubt the wisdom of it, but almost as often celebrate the pleasure of it. His mother read to him from *Smilin' Jack* and *Gasoline Alley*; his father demanded he hold a fork in his fingers instead of his fist; his mother rubbed his legs when they ached; his father placed him upon the back of a stubborn horse with a Mexican name and told him to ride though he could not; his father took him to a cattle tank far away on the prairie where fat green frogs throbbed in the mud and the green grass, wading cattle swished at humming insects, and the redwood windmill creaked in pleasure at the approach of a summer's breath.

The smell and the silence, his father's silence, stirred a quietness in Jack he could like once, remember again, and know as one of the things he would know only once, like the blocks of wood outside his back door.

Returning from the cattle tank, Jack's father began singing, a startling, incredible thing. Years later, Jack could hardly recall his father ever speaking, but never forgot the afternoon he sang, looking straight ahead and driving the faded, borrowed pick-up truck swiftly along the ruts of an eroded road.

"A group of jolly cowboys discussing plans at ease,
Says one, 'I'll tell you something
boys if you will listen please.
I am an old cowpuncher and dressed
in rags you see
I used to be a tough one, and rowdy
as could be.'"

At home that night, Jack's father was as quiet as he always
was, the red beans sliding across his fork in a neat patch, the neat
patch moving expertly into his mouth. From a corner of one eye
Jack watched the splendid grace, the jaw moving only slightly,
the stiffened bristles of the day's beard, the yellow string and
the white tag dangling from the Bull Durham sack in one shirt
pocket. So many things he could not do and could not touch. His
own fork would hardly hold two beans and many times the two
had to be carefully balance, lined in a single file with the juice
splashing down into his plate. Jack asked his mother if she knew
his father could sing. She did not answer. His father did not
appear to hear the question.

Jack himself could not sing, except for two lines of, "You Are
My Sunshine" and most of "Jesus Loves Me This I Know," but
gradually he discovered he had the other abilities. Penniless, he
nevertheless managed to accumulate a treasure in comic books
from a neighborhood playmate by refusing to be a playmate himself until the boy relinquished one of his prize volumes. On the
rare occasions when the friend rebelled at tribute, Jack learned to
discipline himself to hours of solitude, confident his faith in the
friend would result in illustrated reward.

With this friend, Thomas, he accomplished a satisfying triumph one afternoon during a rock fight with the Cornwall brothers and the Cornwall sister. The fight had progressed into several

minutes with never a sign of decision until Jack slipped from behind his own barricade and worked his way around a small hen house. From the far corner he had an unobstructed view of the Cornwall fortress, so formidable in front, bare and defenseless at the flanks. Quickly, before his presence could be discovered, Jack grasped a rounded piece of gravel in his right hand and threw blindly at the Cornwalls, appealing to Sunday School saints for justice. The rock bounded of the forehead of David Cornwall, who fell to the ground screaming and clutching at a mound of visibly swelling flesh. Jack streaked away, victory and escape seeming wings on his heels like the magazine advertisements for tennis shoes. Splashing through a soft corner where the cesspool overflowed in a small, trickling stream, Sweet Afton on this afternoon. Minutes later he was in his own kitchen, contentedly reviewing one of Thomas' former comic books, now his own.

"Did you throw a rock and hit David?" his mother asked.

"No," Jack replied. "I don't know who did."

"I saw you running away."

"I just ran so they wouldn't think I did it."

Lying in his trundle bed that night, Jack thought for a long time about the rock fight, especially about the possibility that it might have been filmed for a newsreel viewing at the Lyric Theater. In a way the fight seemed as important to him as the afternoon his father had taken him to the cattle tank. He was not certain why it was important, but he was not certain about a lot of things he knew. That was a good thing, throwing a rock and striking the mark; a good thing that made lying in his bed so much better than lying in bed had been the night before. That was the part he did not understand: why he could not always feel the way he felt now.

Intruding upon his memory as he stared at the ceiling was the morning he had struck the little girl across the hand with a hatchet. The idea for digging the hole had been the girl's; for

9

him to loosen the earth with the hatchet while she scooped away the result. She should have waited until he had finished before plunging her hand into the hole.

The girl was fortunate the hatchet had been dull, but she had run away, screaming hysterically at the broken skin on her knuckle. Jack's father had not even asked if he had struck the girl with the hatchet, but had used the belt again, the hardest ever. Jack knew that if he had been given a chance he could have told them he had not done the deed the way he had denied striking David Cornwall with a rock, but he was not asked so there had been no opportunity to preserve his feeling for the good feeling, for the Declaration of Innocence. He would remember that among his things to remember, certain it would be as useful as balancing beans on the tines of a fork.

The next morning was loud. A washing machine a block away popped its exhaust, the sound echoing through a huge, empty tin warehouse. Far to the South the sky was blue in the middle, framed by two great fountains of dark smoke—slush pits aflame in the oil fields—breaking the horizon. The Cornwall sister walked down the unpaved street, her little sandals only slight protection against the rough caliche and the collecting heat. She stuck her tongue far out of her mouth and shouted at Jack.

Jack Desbrough stood in the West Texas sunshine, enormous black clouds were breaking the horizon on each side of his vision, his fleece-lined aviator's helmet hot on his head, the goggles pulled down over icy eyes. A stream of sweat flowed down the ridges of his cheeks. He did not have a thin, black mustache, but imagined that he did. A hundred miles away, perhaps a thousand, he could see the future: peaks of great mountains rimmed with crusted blue snow and shrouded by a swirling blood-red mist, haunted by shivering beasts with furred foreheads and wings. It pleased him greatly to be called mean. He remained unafraid.

2

JACK EASILY MASTERED many of the master crafts. Maintaining a fork in the vise of fingers and thumb. Spreading the sugar and salt in a random, invisible plain instead of an impressive alpine mound. He could count to ten with practiced ease. Sing part of "Little Joe the Wrangler." Walk on crushed tin cans. He had tracked the black tarantula to its black hole, climbed to the top of the shingled roof above his home and peered over the rim beyond the boundaries of the town. He could take a thing sheet of paper and a soft-leaded No. 2 pencil and trace in near-perfect detail the curious curves and lines of living and non-living things.

Despite these accomplishments, Jack's parents determined that he would attend school. They enlisted him in the first grade, trading his name and other valuables for a series of questions asked by a young woman, yawning.

The school building was red brick, and surrounded by a wavering line of newly-planted elm trees—all of the trees scrawny and depending for life upon a ditch of water trickling from one tree to the next. The ditch was tended by an old cowboy, remarkably one of the men who had worked with his father on the ranch. The old cowboy was wearing a faded blue jumper and boots with run-down, scruffy heels, bits of leather peeling away from them in random sadness as though marking the years gone by. He was standing, motionless, leaning on a mud-caked shovel, an unlit, newly-rolled cigarette dangling from his lips. Jack passed the old cowboy and entered the schoolyard through a gate protected by an iron-railed cattle guard.

"Hi, boy," the old cowboy said.

Jack's first view of the school ground was interrupted by two huge red buses but when he passed beyond the buses he was struck still by the incredible scene. Children, millions of them, were everywhere. Jack had never imagined school would include so many children. There were clusters of them standing in lines around the slides and swings and the clanging tilt-a-whirl. Individuals eating the edible parts of their lunches. Children crying and laughing and standing awestruck like himself. One fistfight had started, the fight itself obscured by the crowd surrounding the fighters, shouting, screaming, swirling, altering shape as the combat moved from one point to another. Jack's melancholy flaked away, like sickly pearls to be lost and forgotten until they were discovered on other days in his own stomach. He surged into the chaos, eager to learn.

To Jack's amazement, a number of his classmates appeared to be more intelligent than himself. They could numbers he had never heard of; construct chimneyed, neatly-cornered cabins from the Lincoln Logs then and add facsimiles of men and beasts formed with soggy gray clay; recite poems, prayers and nursery rhymes; please the teacher with bouquets of buttercups, sacks of citrus fruit and letters from admiring parents. Jack did not understand why he had never known of these things.

Despite this handicap, Jack quickly assumed class leadership and remained there through the early years of his education. The games he determined to play were the games his classmates favored. In addition to the seasons of marbles and tops and kites dome of them became quite racy, but even the primmest of the little girls in his crowd plunged into the events with feverish enthusiasm, suggesting alternatives that shocked even Buck Jones Hickey, the large, good-natured lad from the Gulf camp who had become Jack's best friend from the day he walked into the schoolyard and who had chewed tobacco, dipped snuff and tasted beer, wine and whiskey. Most of the games were elaborately physical. They included commonsense contests of chance as well as boyish imitations of Sam Baugh, Catfish Smith, Pepper Martin and Flash Harding, the high school fullback who scored six touchdowns against Lamesa despite playing with boils and carbuncles on his back and bottom. They included, as well, instant inventions like the three-month long chase of Tommy Sprattling.

There are, in this state, certain individuals whose presence invites hounding. Insists upon hounding. The explanation for this is readily apparent to those who have ever hounded another individual. They are persons of a peculiar eagerness to please. They plead for love and receive love in its most dramatic form. Their doe eyes seek favor and implore kindness. God-and-man damn them anyhow. Wanting To Be Liked.

Tommy Sprattling was one of these individuals. Each morning recess the boys in Jack's class chased Tommy Sprattling around the playground. They caught him quite easily, knocked him to the ground, permitted him to flee again and then resumed the chase. The slower ones, those who apparently lived with fathers who smoked and were therefore short of wind, dropped steadily behind and only rarely participated in the climax. A lesson they would remember for the remainder of their otherwise noteworthy lives. Some of them fell so far behind they were not so much aware of chasing Tommy Sprattling as they were the fear of stopping. None of the participants pretended they were involved in a game of fun, skill or sense. They knew they needed

13

to catch Tom Sprattling and they did. Dozens of times in a week. Hundreds of times in a month.

One morning, cold in February, Tommy Sprattling momentarily eluded his pursuers by dashing between the gangling swings, grabbing at an idle support chain with one hand as he ran past. He released the swing and the soaring seat, rimmed with metal, sailed back in graceful pendulum and cracked the swift-footed Freddie Frame in the face. Shrapnel from a shattered tooth showered from Freddie's mouth and he screamed and clasped his bleeding lips with both hands.

"I'm sorry, I'm sorry," Tommy Sprattling said, himself in pain and tears. "I didn't mean to. I'm sorry."

Quite suddenly, Jack realized the morning recess was cold. His wrists and hands were red and stiff in the windless chill. He tried to pull them up into the sleeves of his mackinaw by shrugging his shoulders in a certain way he had discovered. He looked away from the whining Tommy Sprattling and the blood leaking between Freddie Frame's lips. "I'm sorry, I'm Sorry," Tommy Sprattling was still saying, still crying.

Donald Rooks, the strongest and meanest boy in class, turned from Freddie to stare with hate at Tommy Sprattling. "Let's get the son of a bitch," he shouted. Instantly, Donald and four others wrestled Tommy Sprattling to the ground, rubbing his nose and mouth into the cold dirt. Jack watched the struggle intently. He had already determined to avoid any of the day's competitions in order to preserve the newness of the boots he was wearing, the leather still shining the way it had done in the box, the trademark still visible on the soles. None of the teachers came outside on cold days so the chastisement of Tommy Sprattling was unlikely to end quickly. Tommy had stopped saying he was sorry and was only crying, his mouth and teeth caked with dirt and his nose and chin becoming raw and streaked with patterns of pink and white skin.

Jack turned to wander away to more entertaining pursuits, then looked back at Donald Rooks, who had recently been establishing his own claim to class power—particularly among a certain group of boys—on the basis of strength and cruelty, a persuasive platform in the early grades and not to be sneered at in the graduate schools of your major universities. Jack returned to the pile of struggling boys and carefully kicked Donald in the left cheek, the grime from his boot unavoidably acting as an abrasive on Donald's young skin; the hard, stiff riding heel catching him just below the jawbone and clicking his teeth together on his fat tongue. Donald immediately began writhing in the dirty grass and dust and his startled followers carefully eased off the back of Tommy Sprattling as they began to realize the game was over for the day. Over forever.

At noon, Jack spent his lunch money on ten rolled-up packages of Guess Whats. The importance of the purchase was diminished by reflections on his immediate future. He sat, alone, on the stack of soda pop bottles behind the tiny school store. The sun was shining coldly and unnoticed and his fingers were freezing as package after package of the Guess Whats revealed prizes for girls or prizes he already possessed in abundance, including three police whistles. A water hydrant had burst during the night and left an incredible frozen arch across his eyesight. Jack shattered the arch with a greasy stick but with none of his usual enthusiasm for exotic experience.

As they walked into the classroom following lunch, Donald Rooks promised Jack he was going to beat the hell out of him after school. Jack realized the promise was not an idle boast. When Donald was called to the backboard to solve an arithmetic problem, Jack took advantage of his position as class slow-reader helper to pass Donald's desk. He removed the papers on top of the desk, stuffing them into his own notebook. Without the papers, Donald was ordered to remain after school

15

and copy them again, a task producing enormous storms of fever and strain on his poor, cloddish brain. The inevitable had been postponed by delayed bully.

Later that afternoon, Jack was returning from the drug store, reading—as he walked—a new *Buck Rogers in the 25th Century* comic book. He was halfway across the deserted block near his home when Donald appeared; leaping from a hole dug amidst the grove of mesquite brush by Jack and his friends and intended more for fortress than for ambush.

"I'm going to whip the hell out of you," Donald shouted, repeating his earlier threat.

He began whipping the hell out of Jack. When Jack was knocked to the ground, he resigned himself to the beating and rolled over on his stomach in order to continue reading. Donald straddled Jack's back, alternately crashing left and right fists into Jack's shoulders and the side of his head.

The beating did not bother Jack especially, although an occasional blow stung one ear or the other and he grew steadily uncomfortable in his position. Donald was displaying no intimations of fatigue and Jack was wondering if the beating would end by nightfall. After several more minutes Jack heard Donald say, "You better not hit me with that."

The beating stopped and Jack looked around, curiously, beyond his left shoulder. Buck Jones Hickey was standing there, a huge slab of half concrete and half rock, plucked from the fortification clutched in both arms like a giant watermelon. The underside of the slab was caked with sharp-edged stones as well as gems of gravel and dark brown clods of mud.

The slab was so heavy Buck Jones Hickey, a strong lad, was staggering as he struggled forward. He walked almost up to Donald and said, apologizing, "It's too heavy to throw." Then he thrust the huge slab away from himself, smashing Donald on the shoulder and head. The force of the splendid boulder, a

16

collaboration of man and nature, knocked Donald off Jack's back and he lay, motionless, under the branches of a winter-bare mesquite bush.

Jack leaped up precisely in time to see the last bit of the sun disappear behind the White Swan Laundry and Dry Cleaners. The twilight glow hung for a moment around the bright faces of Jack and Buck Jones Hickey.

"Thanks, Buck Jones," Jack said, dusting off the cover of his new comic book on his knees.

"Awww," Buck Jones Hickey growled, blushing beneath a rough exterior not unlike the nearby sunset. "You're my best friend."

He was and Jack knew, even then, there would never be another one like him. The two pals walked away, an arm on the other's shoulder.

Donald Rooks, the great bully, watched them depart, enviously. He wished he had a good friend. He wished he could stop crying.

3

SEVEN WEEKS INTO THE SCHOOL YEAR, every year, the evening of the first social event arrived. Portable chairs in the small auditorium were removed and the auditorium and the classrooms directly across the hall were decorated for a Halloween carnival.

Among the older students, those in the fifth and sixth grades, the carnival was accompanied by a noisy collecting of pennies in Mason jars with a slot fashioned in the metal tops. This elementary democracy cost Jack his lunch money every day for a week while he attempted to placate every individual asking him to vote as many times as he pleased at one cent per vote, a campaign tactic for selecting the Halloween queen that he would later see employed in major national elections. The splendor of the decorations—construction paper chains of orange and black, corrugated cardboard booths wrapped in crepe paper—as well as the excitement of his classmates made it obvious the carnival was an occasion of importance as well as expense.

On the afternoon of Halloween, Jack walked the five blocks from the school to his home as he always did. He dazzled his own mind with visualizations for the home-made wonders contained in the booths.

Vaguely, Jack knew that not only must he go, that somehow he would go. By the time he passed the White Swan Laundry, in the next-to-last block from his home, he had accumulated enough resolve to ask his father for permission, a task he dreaded not because he feared his father—although he did—but because he did not like to ask anyone for anything. As soon as the words were out, Jack's new determination was gone with them and he almost turned away—disappointed at himself for his weakness—before his father had time to respond and give him a dime to spend. An unexpected beginning, but nonetheless splendid.

The carnival was all Jack had dared dream. There was noise, a great deal of noise—and loud—faces he had never seen, and laughter. Never before had Jack imagined such happiness. The carnival reminded him of his first day in school, but was even better. The feel of the festival floated through him and gave him a vague sensation of pleasure, although Jack had never learned to be happy or to actually laugh this kind of laughter, idle and with only invisible inspiration.

Jack moved, not slowly, around the arena of color formed by the booths. He determined, as he walked, to spend his dime at the moment of maximum pleasure.

A cakewalk offered intimations of potential. There was music, almost dancing, and the opportunity to win a prize, but the cakewalk was dominated by adults and required more visible presence than he cared or dared to give. A woman in a red kerchief, looking exactly like the grocer's wife would look if she wore a red kerchief, offered to relate Jack's fortune or misfortune, relying entirely upon a knowledge of the wrinkles in the skin of his hand. There was an assortment of things to eat and objects to throw; but in each of three disrupted walks around the entire area, he could see the widest grins of amusement on faces pushing aside a red and white checked oil cloth under a sign which read "Monkey House."

Jack, his mind determined, walked decisively to the woman standing beneath the sign. She was holding another of the Mason jars, nearly filled with coins, her kind face smiling as he approached. Jack gave her his dime quickly; afraid she might talk to him, and slipped behind the oil cloth curtain. The cloth was cool to his touch, so cool he could imagine a chill of anticipation flowing through his body.

The makeshift room surrounding him was small and dark and cast in shadows by a weak yellow globe of light dangling from the ceiling by a long cord. He was alone and the noise outside magnified the silence. Directly beneath the unmasked light bulb was a wooden nail keg decorated by a cardboard sign commanding "Look in Here."

Jack stepped closer to the keg and peered down into the dark chasm. The keg appeared empty at first but then Jack saw, lying on the bottom, a number of small variety store mirrors. In the mirrors he could see the eyes and ears and nose and mouth and the other parts of his face.

He stared at the face in the bottom of the keg for several minutes then walked back into the light and noise. In a kind voice, the kind-faced woman asked Jack if he had seen the monkey. Penniless Jack did not reply. He had been robbed and felt robbed. He had been fooled and felt foolish.

The door to the darkness outside opened to Jack's touch. He began walking toward his home. When he reached the top of the hill, the one place where he could see both his home and his school, he turned and looked back at the yellow light streaming from the schoolhouse window.

"Why would they laugh at that?" Jack wondered aloud. There was no response to his question, but Jack did not worry about that because he had not expected one.

4

A DISEASE had begun to dominate him, but Jack's father still dominated the room and the bed in the room.

The body, now slender, starkly pale and naked looking under the soiled sheet—wrinkled and pushed below the waist in the July heat—still represented a frightening power to Jack. Rib and hip bones strained against the covering skin, white except for the purplish, heavily-stitched, aggravated scar on the left side of the belly. For most of the months of the Disease, Jack's father had struggled to his feet and performed his functions without help except for a broom handle, sawed down and padded with a rubber tip. As the various organs ceased or faltered in their duties, he began to lie entirely on his back and rarely moved except to push the blue sheet down or pull it up whenever a visitor approached.

The visitor was usually from the Lodge or the Court House. He would see an opportunity for charity whenever he sat on the sagging red couch and scraped his feet on the layer of unswept grime on the worn linoleum floor, but Jack's father—as Jack could have told them—rejected the offers of ten dollar bills with harshness and without gratitude. Jack's father was strained of emotion or sentiment and detested any indication of them in anyone else.

Always in the past, Jack's father had been able to do what he chose to do without an awkward apprenticeship or without appearing amateurish, and he wanted dying to be as simple. Like another dying animal, like so many of the coyotes Jack had watched him trap and kill and skin, he wished to be alone and, if not alone, to be avoided.

Once, ignoring the possibility he might not have the knowledge or the equipment, Jack's father had built the house he now lay within. When he decided to move the house, he placed it on rough-hewn skids with a length of pipe and some cursing that defied disobedience even by an inanimate object. Jack, even a very young Jack, had been impressed.

As a younger man, in company with a Brother his equal in contempt for emotion, Jack's father had failed to defeat the Times and together had given their few cattle to a Mexican and walked off their ranch without looking back or ever mentioning the event again; the Brother going to Arizona, then to one of the Philippine Islands and then to somewhere else.

Later, the oil fields bloomed with derricks growing amid bright orange flares by night and dark, growling clouds of smoke from the slush pits by day—the sight Jack liked so much. Other old cowpunchers, friends of Jack's father, joined the roughnecks and drillers and tool pushers from Ranger and Burk, but Jack's father rejected the oil fields as dirty work for dirty men in the same manner he later rejected ten dollar bills. Jack's father forgot he had known these former acquaintances when they began to sit in the Idler's Bar, their grease-soaked clothing smelling of petroleum and used beer, their pockets plump with quarters and softened dollar bills.

Jack's father did not believe an automobile was useful enough to spend money for and never owned a house large enough to avoid having a bed in the living room. He had money only occasionally, but ate steak and cornbread at nearly every evening meal, bought thick magazines, and wore expensive hand-made cowboy boots long after he had given away his spurs and chaps and sold his last pony. Jack wanted the chaps and spurs for his own purposes.

Jack's father himself was the first to be certain of the mistake in the doctor's diagnosis and alone spoke of the Disease by name, fearlessly damning it and God for giving it to him, refusing to disguise it or to discuss the hopes of medical miracle. He seemed to grasp a painful pleasure in telling visitors he would never leave his bed, smiling grimly at their shock in his denial of optimism and cheerful convalescence.

Each week, a barber, with charity in both heart and shears, came to shave Jack's father and Jack listened, interested, as the barber made attempts at conversation, probing—as with his razor—to find a common concern.

"Some folks say a nigger is as good as they are. Well, I always tell them they probably are as good as them... I swallow a lot of hair. All us barbers do. Can't help it... You know it costs more to be poor than rich. Look at banks. They charge you for keeping your money if you don't have very much, but it's free if you do. I had an uncle with hydrophobia and a nephew with Saint Vitus' dance... I said 'Listen you Mobile Alabama son of a bitch, that may be the way you use good whiskey down there but you ain't down there anymore.'"

Usually, Jack's father just closed his eyes, but even when he kept them open he did not respond to the barber's conversation and did not bother to agree or disagree with the philosophies offered free with the free shaves.

As the pain gained possession of him, Jack's father remained silent when he was conscious so only when he fell asleep did his groans become apparent, alternating with his snoring until he was awakened. Jack loved to watch his father during this time. The display of pain was not only entertaining to him, but his father would never have tolerated being watched on other occasions.

Although Jack considered himself weak and cowardly, Jack's father could see that his son had inherited his serenity. In all the months his father was on his back, Jack never inquired about his illness or even appeared aware of it. Jack's father was pleased to see his calmness remain alive, although he sometimes paused in the midst of his agony and attempted to break it, pretending sleep and waiting until Jack tiptoed across the linoleum floor. At the sound of the slightest creaking of the boards, Jack's father swore viciously, "Goddamn boy, don't sneak around here."

Jack quickly learned to avoid these confrontations and did not himself fear his own weaknesses, at least not as much as he feared his father's scorn of them. Within his own thoughts, he remained the principal of hundreds of adventures, rescuer of battered animals, a pal of Our Gang. He could even see himself the equal of his father. A dying father was not likely to interrupt him.

As the end approached, relatives began arriving regularly, seemingly on a prepared schedule, one replacing another in a steady stream. These occasions were holidays for Jack because most of the visitors brought presents or playmates and some of them brought both.

He affected a nonchalance when one of his younger cousins asked if his father was going to die, shrugging off the question and suggesting they talk about something more important. For disturbing him, Jack cheated this cousin out of his cap pistol.

During a particularly sunny afternoon, hotter than one hundred degrees and with no clouds in the sky, an ambulance backed up to Jack's front door. Neighbors, in the shadows of their doorways, watched the peculiar maneuvering of the long, black vehicle over the battered and unwatered grass of the tiny lawn. Jack's father was unusually calm, even for him, and said he would leave after a final cup of coffee. One of the last of his old cowboy friends rolled him a cigarette, one of the tasks Jack had not been able to properly master. A few minutes later, Jack's father was gone, the ambulance slipping quickly and quietly down the street, curls of dust trailing behind in a cheerful fashion, the neighbors still watching in the shadows, the sun still shining.

* * *

That night, Jack's bed was occupied by some of the visiting relatives, so he slept on the couch in the living room. He did not awaken when the telephone rang, but he was awake when he heard his aunt ask, "Will he live through the night?" and he could hear his uncle reply in a whisper.

Jack turned his face into his pillow and spoke to himself in the feathered softness. "I'll have to cry when they tell me," he told himself. He was almost certain he would not be able to do that.

5

WHEN JACK DESBROUGH WAS TWELVE years old, he was apprenticed to a bicycle repairman, a stooped and fat old man, round and hard as a beetle. He was called Bicycle Bob and his shop was named for himself.

Bicycle Bob's weathered face was a network of crevices, wrinkles crossing and counter crossing in patterns approximating an 1890's charting of the Martian canals. In his lapel he wore an American Legion poppy purchased in Hobbs, New Mexico on November 11, 1938. Bicycle Bob had only one true eye, the other space occupied by a false eyeball of a strange blue color with odd markings he declared were an engraving of the continental land masses and the two great snow fields. Although quite adept at bicycle repair, Bicycle Bob preferred to keep a series of young protégés busy at that portion of his business while he devoted a greater, grander part of his time to schemes for surveying the wife of the tinsmith in the building next door; and to continuing a tedious, complicated correspondence with a man in Villa Acuña he identified only as "my agent."

Bicycle Bob occasionally provided his young customers with small items of pornography, booklets purchased in picturesque, frequently-photographed shops on the Mexican border then transported northward in the lunch boxes of butane truck drivers, sandwiched between sandwiches and apple red apples.

Bicycle Bob was vain about his glass eye and one of the first duties assigned young Jack was to regularly patrol the orbiting beauty which would, from time-to-time, whirl around, presenting a stark, chalklike salute instead of the removable globe with its inkling of the Tropic of Cancer and humid climates.

Although Jack did well in keeping this watch, he was less adept at the other tasks delegated him. To grease a chain he would coat half the bicycle's frame in glistening, slippery oil. To contain the air seeping from a punctured inner tube he would wrap a series of patches around the original patch, leaving a tumorous growth bulging over the tire. Even as he observed these inadequacies, Bicycle Bob grew fond of his apprentice and proposed to instruct Jack in the wisdom he had accumulated in a lifetime of fortune hunting and extra-marital adventures. (Extra-marital, that is, for the women involved, as Bicycle Bob himself had never been married).

In rapid succession, Bicycle Bob urged upon Jack bottles and cans of beer, ale and bourbon whiskey, several sizes and shapes of cigars a tin of snuff, a small neighborhood girl named Arlene whose teeth were decorated with metal fillings and fittings that glittered in the sun and fast dazzled Jack.

Bicycle Bob had always been fascinated by the seeding and growth of experience and insisted Jack examine each item carefully before determining those worth pursuing. Bicycle Bob explained that he had never retreated from man or any other natural enemy, once having Jim Thorpe the Immortal Indian tell him he was the hardest-tackling little dickens he had ever seen. Bicycle Bob claimed to have ridden in rodeos, trailed escaped malcontents across trackless and shifting sand dunes, teased a Jehovah's Witness into a fist fight, even fired a bullet into the stomach of a charging German.

"You're a smart boy," he told Jack. "Don't fool around with anything for long. Let the do-gooders do good. You can do better."

On the particular afternoon of that confusing speech, Bicycle Bob closed the shop, clicking the jaws of the padlock together with one hand. As the old man and Jack walked past the tinsmith's shop, Bicycle Bob stopped in the doorway and asked the tinsmith if he knew what a cuckold was. There was no other conversation during the four block's walk to the Driller's Recreation Club where Bicycle Bob had begun teaching Jack to play moon and forty-two and other domino games. "These are social graces, Jack," he explained. "You'll need them. Some girls want a lot more entertainment than Arlene. You'll see. Man with a wristwatch ain't worth a damn if he can't play a game of dominoes."

The Driller's Club was dark, almost as dark as the Lyric Theatre. Cool. Soaked in the heavily-yeasted smell of a thousand spilled glasses of beer. At first, the only noise was the click of shuffling dominoes and the soft whirring of the overhead fans, but after a few minutes a hell of a fist fight broke out between two men dressed like twins in grease-stained khakis and steel-toed driller's boots. Jack could see neither had the hard fisted finesse of the Durango Kid. They scratched and clawed and kicked and slobbered all over one another, fighting like enraged bobcats. One of them ripped through the crotch of the other's trousers and that man, in turn, dug a finger in the corner of the clawer's mouth and attempted to tear the opening wider. When the fight was over, Bicycle Bob told Jack, "No need to get in a fight like that, boy. A man can hire and fire all the fighters he wants right here in this spot. You get to fighting and you forget all the other things I've told you. Wanting to beat the hell out of somebody is what makes a man different from bears and lizards. You got to get over that or you won't have time for anything

31

else. If you do fight, remember I told you to fight anybody but a coward. A coward's the meanest man to beat there is because he throws things and shoots and stabs and hits you with a crowbar. Fight the ones who think they're brave. A smart fellow can whip hell out of that kind."

One day, shortly afterward, a tall, thin man in a brown-striped suit visited Bicycle Bob, talking with him quietly for several minutes in the rear of the shop. Amid the pattern of overturned bicycles, greasy rags and exploded debris there was barely enough room for two men to stand face-to-face, but the stranger was peculiarly constructed, able to bend around shelves and the awkwardly-revolving fan without apparent discomfort. When the stranger departed, Bicycle Bob looked at Jack for several minutes, observing the sturdy lad with the icy eye. "Jack," he asked suddenly, "You ever been to Sunday School?"

Jack, though surprised by the question, replied that he had. He could even recall the principal activity—pasting colored pictures in the corners of a book. "Sure. I've even prayed," Jack answered, anticipating another lesson on experience. "It didn't work."

"Religion can be important," Bicycle Bob said, "I'm surprised I'd forgotten that. You ever been baptized?"

"No," Jack admitted, reluctantly.

"Never too late. You want to be a Baptist don't you?"

"I guess so."

"When I was your age I was the star of a whole revival. I was standing there singing and the preacher kept begging sinners to come up and be saved and telling everybody they were sinners. None of them would go up there so I did. Then, half the crowd come up behind me. There was one pretty little girl there and after church I asked her what rotten things she had done, but she wouldn't tell me. Girls don't brag much, but I've known some of them to do some rotten things. That don't make any difference anyhow. There's a revival meeting tonight and you might as well start. Listen to the music and at the end when they start singing sad songs you go on up and tell the preacher you want to be saved and baptized. You can't be one without the other. I don't think. He'll tell you what. I've been saved numberous times."

That evening, Jack pedaled up to the Immanuel Baptist Church on his racing bicycle. The fenders were stripped away and bare rubber cleaved the wind as he struggled through the sandy streets. He was barefooted so grease from the heavily-oiled sprocket made his toes slippery on the worn-to-metal pedals. The church was a long, white wooden building located at the corner of two unpaved streets. Bulbs in the street lamps had been shattered; two of them by Jack himself. The corner was entirely dark except for a glow from the opened windows and a bare fixture hanging above the front porch of the church.

The night was warm. Quiet. Jack pedaled silently up to the row of windows parallel to Mabel Street. He stopped in the darkness between two of the windows and looked inside at the congregation singing. "Standing, standing, standing on the promises..." The piano was loud, breaking above the voices in crashing waves. Jack was thinking of riding away and telling Bicycle Bob he had been saved and baptized when he heard a voice coming from a nearby clump of evergreen shrubs.

"Why don't you go on in?" the voice asked. Jack, thinking he was being addressed by angels, could not reply. Finally he discovered hidden among the shadows, a man standing with a glowing cigarette in one hand. The man, the same stranger who had approached Bicycle Bob earlier in the day, walked toward Jack and Jack could see he was wearing a dark suit, his white socks twinkling like crawling stars in the darkness.

"I'm Mister Ralph Preston," the man said, "and we'd be glad to have you share our fellowship." Jack's brain fairly reeled with excuses tumbling over themselves; but before he could employ them, Mister Ralph Preston clasped him around the shoulders.

Jack permitted himself to be directed through the front door and into a pew at the rear of the auditorium. Mister Ralph Preston sat next to Jack, his thin triangular nose and his octagonal spectacles shining in the light and in the glances from those seated nearby. Jack recognized a few faces, mostly boys he hated at school. Mister Ralph Preston put an arm around Jack's shoulders again and told him to open his heart to Jesus and Jesus would enter. All of Jack's sins, no matter how black and pestilential, would be washed away in the precious blood of the lamb. He said these things loudly, looking around and smiling at certain acquaintances. Jack was embarrassed but said he would open his heart. He knew Bicycle Bob would want him to do that.

The preacher spoke of the powers of God, mentioning football players who scored touchdowns against impossible odds as evidence of the faith. He spoke of boils and carbuncles, a story already familiar to Jack, who knew about the Lamesa game. He related a number of anecdotes about the named and unnamed, the gospel gossip that averts so much dependence on death-bed recitals. He said God was all things to all men, nourishment for the famished, swiftness for the slow-afoot, strength for the cowardly. "Confused," Jack thought, recalling Bicycle Bob's Lesson on Fighting.

At last, the invitation came. The preacher was standing on the floor before the pulpit. The congregation was singing softly, "Just as I am without one plea…" The preacher saying, "Every eye closed, every head bowed…"

Jack looked around to count those who were disobeying. Suddenly, he lurched from the pew and onto the red carpet leading to the preacher, the bristles tickling his greased feet. "A new soul for the Lord," shouted Mister Ralph Preston, walking directly behind Jack and smiling radiantly as the curious turned to watch the parade.

I want to be baptized tonight," Jack said, looking up at the baptistery: a metal tank behind the choir loft and in front of a painted background showing a blue river between green, shaded banks, the painted waters flowing down into the tank. On a visit to East Texas, Jack had once seen just such a river, but had not been permitted to wade in the waters because of his uncle's fear of the cotton mouth and the water moccasin.

"Praise the Lord," shouted the preacher. "This young man is ready for baptism. He has surrendered his soul to the Lord. The battle is won. The rejoicing has just begun."

"You can't be baptized tonight," Mister Ralph Preston whispered. "We don't run water in the tank Thursday nights."

The next day, Jack told Bicycle Bob he would not be able to work for a few days because he would be baptized on Sunday and, on the following Tuesday, would depart for a youth encampment at Big Spring. "Jesus Christ," Bicycle Bob said. "I told you to get some religion not become a goddamned disciple." During the afternoon, Jack—experiencing religious discipline—gave Arlene and her fancy slit only cursory examination.

The encampment was a hand-crafted oasis on the desert. The sun, untouched by clouds or trees, blazed directly downward, hovering close by during the entire day. There were splashes of greenery—weeds and mesquite bushes—on the sides of a dry, irregular ravine, much higher on one side than the other. Campsites of the gathering church groups were established along the sandy bottom of the ravine. Homely permanent buildings—the chapel, the cafeteria—were on the higher level which continued on as a plateau supporting the countryside for hundreds of unseen miles. Jack and his new friends spread their blankets near the counselor's tent, a few yards from the main avenue trailing along the ravine's bottom before continuing as a path to the plateau above.

The first afternoon was occupied by a preaching service devoted to describing the horrors of Hell followed by supper and then another preaching service devoted to measuring the length of those horrors should an unsaved sinner be consigned there. Later that night, Jack was lying on his back near a boy trying to look into the counselor's tent. Jack was staring straight up into the moon thinking of the way baptism had saved him from a life of hell in Hell. Suddenly, a peace-shattering scream resounded from the opposite side of the ravine and loud, squishy plops began to thud all around him.

"It's the Big Lake bunch. They're bombing us with gourds," someone shouted. The boy near Jack grabbed a rock and threw the stone blindly into the darkness. Gourds continued to rain everywhere, followed by shouts of triumph and cries of dismay and heavy, running footsteps possessing no visible stepper. The darkness turned into a tableau of aforementioned hellfire: meat and seeds from broken gourds splashing on beds and panicking younger boys caught in hideous crossfire.

"Let's get the bastards," Jack heard a voice whisper. Instantly, Jack and the whisperer, Billy Bob Whitlock, charged into the darkness, risking the unbroken barrage of gourds and rocks. Jack and Billy Bob dashed down the ravine, past other startled campers stirring at the sounds of the raid. At the Big Lake camp site, Jack and Billy Bob urinated onto some of the bedding, threw dirt and twigs into the other bedrolls, kicked up the stakes on the counselors' tent, and then fled back down the path and into the night.

* * *

"The devil is never far away," the preachers said at the next morning's service. "He manipulates his power in many ways, some of the strange to us. The boys who so disturbed the camp

36

last night should know the Lord was ashamed. The Jesus wept over the things they did. They fell into the devil's sway and you could hear him chuckling over the countryside. The Lord never intended his gourds to be thrown all over a ravine, splattering the clothing of some of our fine ladies. He would weep at the sight of bedding so shabbily soiled."

A few hours later, the entire encampment—almost a hundred boys—departed on the traditional two-mile hike across the plateau. The ground was already hot to the touch, the entire desert vacated by every living thing except a few grasshoppers and singing locusts. After the first half mile; some of the weaker, younger boys began to complain of the heat, to plead for water or Kool-Aid. At the end of the Mile's walk, at the turning point, the entire party had taken up the complaint.

"Water," they cried. "Let's stop and pray for water."

"God, we've got to have water," exclaimed a fat boy, sweat darkening his shirt, a rare pinkness appearing on the bridge of his nose and creeping across both chubby cheeks. The incredible ordeal continued through the last mile, Jack confident he would die but too proud to whine, too tired to applaud Billy Bob when that worthy spat cotton on a rock and side armed the rock barely past a counselor's plodding head.

Only one faucet was available for the thirsty boys and they stood impatiently in line, drinking their bloated fill of cold water. Jack was near the end of the line, doubly thirsty when he finally arrived at the spigot. He gulped in a great quantity of water, and then walked away, his cheeks bulging with even more water, streams from each side of his mouth forming a boiling cataract at chin point and then tumbling in waterfall down his chest.

During the night, Jack and Billy Bob and most of the others, even the Big Lake boys—all deathly ill from the water ration—vomited in the ravine, mostly around the path the counselors would take the next morning. Still sick, they lay on their pallets in the hot sun throughout the early service, refusing all pleas to rise and shine and be healed. Early that afternoon, the entire group was loaded into the back of a cattle truck, only casually swept from recent business, and returned to Odessa.

* * *

"Bicycle Bob," Jack said, his toes rubbing luxuriously against the steel in his new driller's boots, the gift of Bicycle Bob and Arlene, "I fought a coward at the camp and all he did was cry. He didn't do anything but cry."

Bicycle Bob, who was digging a hole to bury a poisoned dog left on his doorstep by the tinsmith's wife, threw a shovelful of earth at Jack's feet. "Boy," he said, "some people claim the whole world is rotten. Look at it right there. Full of worms."

6

FOR ALL HIS LOYALTY, Jack Desbrough one day found it necessary to discard Buck Jones Hickey as his best friend. Buck Jones remained as strong as ever and perpetually valorous, but he was also a bumbling, roughhewn lad and as Jack began to develop in poise and prowess he grew all to conscious of his friend's shortcomings. Jack was determined, however, to spare Buck Jones any embarrassment or bitterness and, as a result, never bothered to tell him he was no longer his best friend or rarely even talked to him again.

The particular duties of friendship were assumed, quietly, by Max Murphy, remarkably like Jack himself in manner, size and instinct. Max Murphy was also Bicycle Bob's nephew. In his role as Jack's employer and Max's uncle, Bicycle Bob could exercise his dubious talent for scout mastering without the loyalty oaths, the natty uniforms, the good deeds the unit citations and the other extraordinary crap of boy scouting. Because of his old face and his advanced age Bicycle Bob was frequently mistaken for an adult, although he rarely performed as one. Whenever he accompanied Jack and Max on explorations or demolitions, Max's mother would sometimes call Jack aside and ask him to watch over both of them.

Except on the rare days of rain or cold and the less rare days when the sand was blowing through town, Bicycle Bob did not like to remain in his shop. Frequently the only work even attempted there was accomplished on days of adverse weather—too hot, too cold, too windy—so that the prospect of regular employment grew steadily more repulsive to both Jack and Max.

On many days, Bicycle Bob would padlock the premises and the three of them would ride their customer's bicycles to the edge of town, leave the bikes under a large mesquite tree and walk across the browning prairie to a nearby cattle tank. The walks were hot and dusty, but the effort was always rewarded. They would rest in the shade of the chinaberry trees for a long time, then one of them would wander off to shoot a jackrabbit (there was only one gun among them, a single-shot rifle of antique appearance and ability). Once they had a warm carcass in their midst, they had no reservations about spending the remainder of the time sprawled about the grassy bank. Bicycle Bob, who felt obliged to exert and elderly influence continued to issue his articles of advice, instructing Max as well as Jack.

"Boys, I know you've heard a lot of things," he would say, for one example, "but you don't have to believe them all. Besides, a good hairy palm will probably do you some good when you go to play baseball."

Once, when the three of them were returning from a tank, Bicycle Bob stopped to show them how to build a campfire with a Ronson cigarette lighter, first placing the smaller twigs in a pile and then the larger ones atop them. "Woodcraft," he explained. Bicycle Bob had barely ignited the fire when a rattling Packard automobile approached, dust swirling behind the vehicle and clouding the prairie. The Packard stopped near them and a deputy sheriff wearing Tony Lama cowboy boots with walking heels dismounted. His gun was stuck into a holster and the holster stuck into his hip pocket. He had the confident walk of a man with just that sort of treasure within his reach.

"What the hell are you doing?" he asked Bicycle Bob.

"Starting a fire," Bicycle Bob said. "We were getting cold."

"In this goddamn heat? Who the hell are you kidding?"

"Well, it was only a little fire."

"Listen," the deputy said. "The owner of this property says some kids've been shooting the hell out of his cattle. Now I didn't see you shooting no cattle but it's illegal as hell to go around starting fires on this property. You're trespassing. I want you to get the hell off this property and don't come back. Give me your names."

"I'm John J. Pershing and these are my aides," Bicycle Bob said.

"Listen Pershing, you guys get the hell of this property. I'll be back to see you stay off."

The three of them watched the deputy drive away, steering neatly along old, rarely-used wagon ruts.

"Gripey son of a bitch," Max said.

"Boys, you have to have respect for John Law," Bicycle Bob said. "The man was doin' his job and you got to have respect for a man doing his job. What we ought to do is do him a favor. Make some work for him. Here, if we can get these weeds blazing up right across here we might get us a whole little prairie fire going. I thought so. Always dry this time of the year... Spreading quicker than I thought. Maybe we better walk a little faster."

The fire sputtered briefly, then flashed brilliantly across the plain. Mother Nature and the Ronson cigarette lighter in crackling, roaring, holocausting co-operation. Jack and Max walked backwards, admiring the smoking desert, breathing in the smell of burning grass deep into their lungs.

Despite the success of the fire, neither of the lads could escape a feeling of melancholy the following day. The visits to the cattle tank were ended for a lifetime, joined to the list of the vanishing pleasures of their vanishing boyhood. Bicycle Bob, watching them sit quietly in the doorway, recognized the ache. He could feel the same ache himself and all his efforts at cheering them seemed tangled with failure. He bought them a nudist magazine, but they were only momentarily distracted. He took them to the county courthouse to shout insults at the drunks in the third floor jail, but their shouts went unanswered.

Finally, reluctantly, Bicycle Bob realized he would have to make some dramatic gesture to restore the boys' faith in himself and an entertaining world. He promised them a camping trip to the saline lake near Grandfalls, a salty, shallow pond surrounded by clumps of cedar trees and sweating couples, coupled.

Bicycle Bob did not often drive, but on the occasions when he did he drove with all his might, keeping the wheels rolling with manipulations of the steering mechanism, pushing the accelerator to the floor as hard as he could, stepping on the brake with the same effective force: going when he was going, stopping when he was stopping.

Fifteen miles outside Odessa, he veered off the highway and into the bar ditch to run over a dust-flaked rattlesnake. "There was a goddamned lesson for you boys," Bicycle Bob said, cigar clutched in the middle of his mouth, the words coming out on both sides of the smoke, as though illustrating his lecture like comic strip balloons. "Man has the power of life and death over other animals. That snake wouldn't have come out of the ditch after us would he? But man is something special. That's why he has to blow his nose and catches rheumatism."

Twelve miles later, Bicycle Bob drove through a flock of squawking White Leghorn chickens. Blood, feathers and intestines exploded over the windshield. Bicycle Bob turned on the wipers and the radio.

"I made a kid into a religious fanatic once," Bicycle Bob
ignoring the splotches of blood and feathers clinging t
clicking wipers. "I never meant to do it, but things work (
way sometimes. We were working on his bicycle and I
fingers through the sprockets. He commenced to yelling for
to get them out. It was me that done it, but he give all the cre
to God and he came out a new man when his fingers was healea.
Before that he had been a mean little bastard. Once I know he
poured gasoline on a cow's hoofs and set them on fire. After
that day in the shop he was afraid of any kind of fire, thinking it
might be for him. What a little bastard he used to be."

The lake was crowded, but Bicycle Bob eased his automobile
to the edge of the water between two families spreading picnic
lunches. The two families comprised one larger party and were
loudly rude about the intrusion, but Bicycle Bob ignored them
and took off his trousers, exposing his long white underwear and
long white feet. Bristling white hairs, like weird cactus thorns,
were growing on the roof of his large toes. Two of the men from
the picnicking families approached and one of them—a tall,
muscular bruiser wearing a letter jacket with several stars, stripes
and various balls decorating a huge green "M"—shouted, "What
the hell are you doing?"

"I'm wading," Bicycle Bob said, wading.

"You get out of there or we're going to whip your old ass," the
young man said. "What the hell's the matter with you? Are you
drunk or doped up or something?"

Bicycle Bob bowed his head and began talking, sadly, "These
are my grandsons," he said. "I promised their mother—their
mother's sick—I promised to show them a good time. They're
just poor boys who wanted to do a little swimming. Their mother
wanted them to and I thought I'd bring them out here."

The young man in the decorated "M" softened his angry voice.
"Listen Pop, I didn't mean for you to leave, but you put your

pants back on and go somewhere else. My mom is here too and I don't like her seeing somebody run around in their underwear. It don't look good."

Bicycle Bob waded out of the water and slapped the young man on the shoulder. "All right, son," he said gently, "I didn't mean to be offensive."

Bicycle Bob climbed back into the automobile where Jack and Max still sat and slowly backed away from the scene. The young man was smiling now and waving goodbye, telling his family something about a "good-hearted old fellow." Suddenly, Bicycle Bob wheeled his vehicle around, the skidding rear wheels scattering sand, gravel, and the remaining chicken feathers on the family gathering.

Jack and Max looked back but could not see anything. A cloud of dust hung over the picnickers, obscuring their reaction. Bicycle Bob left the same trail of dust behind as he skirted the edge of the lake, bushes and small salt cedar trees on each side of the primitive trail clawing at the metal sides of the automobile.

"Only way to handle some sons of bitches," Bicycle Bob said, his face reflecting an image of pleased reflection about previous sons of bitches he had handled.

Several minutes later, the three of them stopped again, this time to establish their position for the night. While Bicycle Bob was making coffee over their campfire, Jack and Max wandered off along the lakeshore. A half mile away they stopped to watch a young couple standing waist deep in the water. The boy was behind the girl, his arms around her and one hand wiggling into the bottom half of her bathing suit. The yes of both appeared glazed over and they ignored Jack and Max even when the adventurous pair tossed pebbles and splashed small plumes of water on them. The boy continued his struggle, the girl stood quietly, like a well-stanchioned cow.

Bored, the two boys returned to the camp. Bicycle Bob fed them a Vienna sausage sandwiches and drank several cups of coffee, his underwear gradually becoming the only brightness in the otherwise darkening county.

"Boys," he said. "I'll sleep in the car. You take the blankets and make yourselves comfortable out here under the stars. Only way to camp when you get right down to it."

Jack and Max lay together, each of them wrapped in a thick blanket. Bicycle Bob was soon snoring, but shortly afterward the noise of his snoring was drowned by the sound of the suddenly shifting wind. The first cold, unexpected norther of the late autumn had blown into the area from chilled mountainsides hundreds of miles distant. Stars disappeared from the sky and cold become the only reality. Bicycle Bob got out of the automobile and took Max's blanket. "You wrap together boys," he said cheerfully, "this is what camping's all about."

The old man returned to the automobile and rolled up the windows. At intervals during the night, Jack and Max heard him start up the motor and idle the engine for several minutes. "He's got the heater on," Max said, "The old bastard."

"He's your uncle," Jack said, shocked.

"Uncle Bastard then."

The boys clung together for warmth, but the night was a miserable experience. They became convinced they were freezing and if the other had not been there would have begun crying.

At daylight they were surprised to be alive though not especially grateful for the blessing. As Bicycle Bob began the drive home, he could see Jack and Max were angry. He attempted to win them back, promising to pay for tattoos and telling them amusing stories and making flattering references to their hardiness, but they did not respond.

Their boyish days were over, dead—if they were not—and Bicycle Bob drove on. He drove as he always did, realizing there was no reason, now, to slow down.

7

JACK CONTINUED the regularly-scheduled contest of growing up in much the way anyone else might have accomplished the feat, a trifle more confidently perhaps but otherwise unarmored.

Often, stirring around in his tin-roofed room—which almost connected with the remainder of the family home—Jack would pore over stories of the boyhoods of Midwestern youths. Paragraphs describing sycamore-lined boulevards especially fascinated him although, when he stepped outside and the fierce sun splashed upon his handsome head, he realized Roxanna Avenue would not soon be lined with sycamore trees. That unpaved street was sometimes skinned down to a rare smoothness by the county maintainer, but shortly afterward this new, brown and splendid earth returned to sand. Up and down the avenue he could hear the angry cries of dismayed bicycle riders as they floundered on a street-corner dune and began the slow, inevitable fall on their asses. He considered the other scenes that made this street unfadeable in his memory. The day of the flash flood when he and assorted friends, acquaintances and strangers had floated in the muddy waters on huge house-moving timbers provided by one of the fathers. The afternoon another of the fathers had used a winch truck to bloodily dehorn a milk cow. The day a neighborhood kid attempted to gain entry into their newly-dug cave by promising to provide his sister for them to mount, embarrassing the lot of them because they had already grown weary of her services—she was even then in the cave— but were too manly to admit it. The one-room plywood house occupied by a family whose members produced a stench so strong Jack had to hold his breath to knock on the door during the two occasions he had been dispatched there.

Jack could not imagine any of these things being a part of an Indiana boyhood. Whenever he thought of them, the unfairness of his life descended around him as certainly as the red-and-white striped shirt he habitually wore. He knew of no reason he should be on Roxanna Avenue—with its hot sand and dazed residents—when all over Indiana boys of his age were cavorting in old swimming holes and playing football across lawns over-flowing with cool green grass. Joyful Midwestern cries occupied his daydreams so intensely Jack even considered conveying the passion to Max Murphy, his best friend. Only the awareness his enthusiasms were rarely contagious prevented him from doing so.

To his dismay, Jack did once make the mistake of revealing the dream to a visiting uncle; mentioning it, as a matter of fact, several times, usually during the evening meal. Jack had directed his appetite almost entirely toward dry cereal; corn flakes, shredded wheat, puffed rice, bran flakes with and without raisins, as well as variations and combinations of these and other milled products. His preoccupation with cereal boxes and words like thiamin and riboflavin annoyed Jack's uncle, but when Jack gave them up to talk about Indiana his uncle was annoyed even further.

"What I'd like to do," Jack suggested to his mother, "Is move our whole house up there or maybe plant a lot of sycamore trees around here."

"You crazy little shit," Jack's uncle shouted. "What the hell do you know about sycamore trees? For all you know they cause elm disease." The uncle lapsed into adult anger and slammed his cornbread into his plate, scattering beans all over the kitchen floor. Jack admired the gesture well enough, but in his gravest imaginings he did not think his Indiana contemporaries had fathers or uncles who called them crazy little shits.

Despite the contempt his suggestion had aroused, Jack did not give up on his plan. Unknown to his uncle, his mother, Bicycle Bob, Max Murphy, Arlene, or anyone else, he quietly determined to live an Indiana boyhood; preparing himself for the day when he would stroll through a typical small Midwestern town and feel as though he had lived there throughout his life.

Quite obviously he would not be able to assemble a typical small-town Indiana gang of close chums. For one thing, Jack had only Max Murphy as an intimate friend. Max, a versatile sort, could doubtless have made a Midwestern place for himself except that his interests were now limited to excavating an enormous cave in the mostly sandy alleyway. He was constantly dragging up large pieces of lumber, scraps of sheet metal, and anything else he could find to use as a covering for the elaborate tunnels, rooms, nooks and culs-de-sac that comprised one of the most impressive feats of engineering in south Odessa history. One Sunday afternoon, while a Mexican family was away on a fishing trip, Max managed to remove the plywood paneling from the family's trailer, leaving the furnishings naked beneath the framework. He covered the latest of the cave's major rooms with the siding and hid the crime under several inches of dirt. Upon its return from Red Bluff, the Mexican family was stunned at the disappearance of their home and vowed to never leave for a mess of catfish again.

The other lads in the neighborhood were even less promising than Max. Billy Fry was friendly enough, agreeable to anything, but his company was rarely welcome. Attending a movie with him was a horror. He was afflicted with a nervous disorder—generally, though erroneously, identified by various mothers as St. Vitus' Dance. His affliction caused young Billy to squirm in an irritating fashion, clutch at his salivating lips and utter, "ooooo, goddamn, ooooo, goddamn," at five minute (approximate) intervals, attracting the attention of mean ushers and bullying old ladies. In addition, he was a perpetual victim of the sort of accidents that made other boys deny he was a friend. He had, to cite one instance, sat in a fresh cow patty then reported to the schoolyard with the decoration still on the seat of his pants.

Jesse Turnbow was a tall, skinny boy with considerable athletic prowess. Yet, no matter how splendidly he played, he seemed always to be rewarded with disaster. Once, stealing home plate to try and win a baseball game, he was smashed in the mouth by a teammate striking out. Another afternoon, during a football game, he evaded a charging lineman, sprinted down the sideline and was on his way to the game's winning touchdown until he dashed through a pile of smoldering leaves. One of the live embers lodged in a moccasin and Jesse Turnbow collapsed, screaming and crying. He was doubly jinxed. A man whose talent was tragedy. Hardly the sort to share a harsh Midwestern winter with.

Jack could see he would have to make the venture alone. The prospect did not disturb him in the least. If the truth were as certain as other things one could realize he did not savor the prospect of sharing Indiana's pleasures with the residents on Roxanna Avenue. Preferably, he would awaken with a completely new family, living on a quiet street interrupted by casual song birds and a smiling postman. His friends would be hearty Midwestern types with boyish grins on their faces and a series of bully adventures and pleasant times the only items in their future. The West Texas sun and the Panhandle dust would be as foreign to them as the sighting of Himalayan beasts. Their eyes would never have to close to keep out the blowing sand; only for naps and nine hours of dream-blessed slumber. In the morning, their mothers would awaken them by touching them gently on a shoulder and telling them their hearty Midwestern breakfasts were prepared. Their teeth would gleam from effort-less polishings and they would never have stomach cramps or bowel movements.

Occasional realities would intrude into these reveries and when they did Jack made no serious attempt to evade them. He realized his Midwestern father would have a few chores for him to attend to before he would be permitted to join his keen companions for a malted milk at the soda shop. He imagined one of these chores would be setting fire to piles of previously raked sycamore leaves and then standing guard over them to see that they did not do whatever it was burning leaves were inclined to do, especially lodge in the shoes of sprinting comrades. Since there were no trees around his home on Roxanna Avenue, Jack's own chores involved somewhat more esoteric ventures appointed by his mother or, more recently, his uncle. He seemed to spend a lot of time shoveling chicken shit out of the chicken yard, making room for more of the same which he would also have to shovel. However, his principal occupation was chopping away at the goatheads, prolific and perilous week with monster sticker buds threatening to engulf the block and possibly the entire south side of town.

One afternoon, Jack had hoed and raked a stack of the goat-heads almost to the point of relaxation. He leaned on the hoe handle and, as he looked down Roxanna Avenue, he could see the gradually approaching form of Geneva Foster, a tall, thin girl believed to be stricken with tuberculosis. There was only the noise of a tiny dust devil forming in his front yard, disturbing mesquite bushes freshly blooming fuzzily in the background. Although Jack had no particular fondness for tubercular females, he could easily imagine himself guarding a stack of smoking leaves and watching, with approval, the approach of his beloved, typically Midwestern girlfriend.

As Geneva came nearer, Jack slitted his eyes to better view his own vision and Geneva grouched out, "What are you looking at, you goofy son of a bitch?"

Jack, as usual, was not in the least disturbed by the rude remark. He was mentally hardened to overlook that sort of crap. During his reflections, though, he determined that no female who called him goofy would ever be a girlfriend of his. He tried to place Geneva in a Booth Tarkington setting, but he did not try very hard.

Except for rare encounters like this, Jack was generally left to his own daydreams and continued the preparation for his elaborate boyhood. He coaxed his mother into financing two lessons on the Hawaiian steel guitar, began running laps around his property, and mailed off for a cluster of booklets telling him how to mold a mighty back, mighty chest, mighty arms, mighty legs and a mighty grip. As he gained strength, endurance and manly character, he also gained in self-respect and occasionally even wondered if Indiana would be good enough for him. One particular afternoon, he whipped both Max Murphy and Rollo Schmittou, toughest of the Schmittou twins. There was no danger involved in either of the battles, though they were fought as seriously as they could have been. Jack realized there would have occurred a display of considerable ill will had either Max or Rollo ever gained the upper hand. So long as they were losing, they maintained a tight-lopped grimace they passed off as laughter and good cheer—an item of the public psychology not at all lost on Jack Desbrough, who had nevertheless always found a charitable attitude to be one of the things he could most easily afford.

In compliance with this remark, another noteworthy incident: During a school ground wrestling match Jack lost his pocket knife, a neat instrument encased in a handle composed of hundreds of chips of color, once the knife of his grandfather. He grievously missed the knife and two or three weeks later saw it being used in a whittling fashion by a slight boy of only remote acquaintance. The discovery of the knife in another's hands aroused a panther of emotion in Jack's mind. He knew, beyond the shadow of a doubt, the knife was his own. The odds against another such splendid, aging handle showing up in one school-yard at one time were so remote as to be incalculable. Yet, Jack could not bring himself to accuse the knife wielder of stealing. For one thing he was much stronger than the thieving bastard so both an unwillingness to be accused of bully-like tendencies and the instinct to avoid injuring another individual's feelings entered into his calculations.

Jack's natural kindness won the day and he soon devised a way out of the dilemma. He fashioned an ingenious mechanism of two-by-fours, nailing the shorter on top of the longer and then shaping a handle of the surplus extending from the longer plank. The result was a strong, thick, club-like club. Armed with this device, Jack lurked in the shrubbery along the knife thief's route from school to his home. He pulled his red-and-white striped shirt over his head and then buttoned part of the shirt across his face, an appearance he imagined left him looking like a Berber bandit. When the thief passed, Jack stepped behind him, stunned him silly and relieved him of the knife and the pitiful remainder of his lunch money. Jack did not really crave the piddling change, but chose to make the deed appear the work of desperate robbers, probably Mexican kids who were known to crave lunch money more than dope or lunch. The thief's tears dripped into the sand, making mud.

Although Jack felt certain he had handled the entire affair with a minimum of embarrassment for all concerned, he also wondered about its effect on his plans for a typical Midwestern boyhood. He had, by this time, already given up on ever moving to Indiana, but nevertheless continued to harbor the dream of "Indiana-of-the-Mind" on the prairies of West Texas. He realized his violent deed represented an enormous detour on the route and, as he so often did, he took the problem to Bicycle Bob, his mentor.

The grouch-stricken philosopher, grieved by the departure of the tinsmith's wife to her Arkansas homeland, was not entirely in the mood to comfort another, even his arch-apprentice. His own heart was sick and the fantastic flowering tattoos of his arms—pinks and blues, tiny roselets and bluebells in a filigree of dainty black lace and ribbons—were fading and dying, slowly being replaced by a field of freckles and liver spots. Considering his state of mind, it would be impossible to accurately evaluate the things Bicycle Bob told Jack that afternoon.

"Sometimes I'm afraid there really isn't a Hell," Bicycle Bob said, "and all the bastards are going to get away with it. You've got to believe in Hell, boy. There has to be something worse. Don't stay scared. It's only life."

Jack, Loveable Jack, had no objection whatsoever toward believing in Hell. He wondered, however, how he would ever adapt that device to his life. He could feel himself slipping further away from Typical. Not slipping. Falling.

8

HIGH SCHOOL, for Jack, was quite like a three-year holiday interrupted by occasional holidays. The years were a time of games and promenades, flag raisings and cheers in the night, fist fights and the other frolics that prepare a young man for graduating from high school. There were classes, to be sure, but Jack had long been a regular reader of the Fort Worth Star-Telegram's Sunday comic and sports sections, had almost memorized the usable portions of the Open Road for Boy's Handbook. He had endured several hundred hours of Bicycle Bob's lectures on everything. Consequently, he had no more difficulty with his studies than he had with tying his shoe laces, although the latter task was certainly not as simple as might be immediately assumed. Jack's ruined laces more resembled a series of connected knots rather than genuine strings. Coaxing enough slackness from them to manufacture a neat bow was no trivial accomplishment.

To be entirely accurate an assortment of minor incidents, in combination, contrived to keep Jack's high school days from being entirely euphoric. The most serious of these was in the matter of dress. Jack and his contemporaries all wore Levis, white shirts, and belts with large silver buckles; each individual conspiring to look as much like the other as possible. As fashion would have it, the Levis had to be shrunken to the tightest possible functioning. The shrinking method involved putting them on when brand new, watering them down thoroughly with a garden hose, and then lying in the sun until they were dried to a proper, fashionable fitting. As luck would have it, this shrinking process seemed to concentrate on Jack's pelvis, so the pressure on his gonads was terrific. Often, the pain would become so intense he would surreptitiously look around at his classmates, dozing in the warm spring, to see if he could detect a similar suffering. There never seemed to be any, leaving Jack with spiritual doubts, wondering what sort of deity could single him out for aching balls. During these periods of his childhood yearning for a typical Indiana boyhood would return, occasionally replaced by a similar enthusiasm for a New England schooling where he would pass merry, snow-flecked classmates clad in sensible corduroys and tweeds, their testicles cozy and comfortable.

In addition to dress, there was an early problem with social standing. Neither Jack nor Max Murphy could afford the accoutrements and incidentals for even a modest date. They had no transportation, beyond their own wits, and both were keenly aware of the obstacles this placed between them and potential sweethearts. Arlene, of course, was always available, which—come to think of it—was exactly what was wrong with Arlene. The boys retained a great affection for her charms but could readily see that attaching too much faith in them would be a social blunder of the worst possible sort. "Keep the hell away from us," they told her, not unkindly.

Geneva was the only other neighborhood possibility and on the scale of acceptance she gave Arlene the status of homecoming queen in a pristine state certified and attested by notary public. Although Jack and Max agreed, along with all their acquaintances, that they would draw the line at nothing—"If she's got thick ankles throw a flag over her ankles"—they privately admitted there was something definitely unattractive about Geneva's tubercular body. For a few months they deftly snaked through the weeds and mesquite bushes in the vacant lot next door to Geneva's home, then through the weeds and mesquite bushes in the lot that was her home, to peer at her undressing antics. Frequently, she had caught them and dared them to come inside and "do something about it," but neither of the boys wanted to be first and both would have despaired at being second, especially to one another. As Geneva grew more emaciated they gave up the sport as both troubling and depressing. When she died, they congratulated themselves for having avoided her germed clasp.

Some good, however, had evolved from this experience. As a result of their nights prowling around Geneva's bedroom window, Jack and Max had grown sly and tricky. Whenever a school function was in progress they were there to enjoy the scene, as unseen as they were uninvited; but always there, wearing black shirts and black trousers, sitting in the underbrush and listening to the music leaking through opened windows and doors. When they tired of this pastime, they crawled away in the puddles of shadow, rifling cars for items they needed more than the owners and regularly setting upon the tennis and golf players and other fruity types, knocking the hell out of them and making their escape through the hedges and over the towering chain-link fences surrounding the tennis courts.

Once, while they were in the process of kicking crap out one of the tennis stars, preparatory to throwing his trousers on the gymnasium roof, they were chased away by a gang of ruffians, some of them still wearing their tennis shoes but most of them dressed in sharp sports coats, creased trousers and shined dancing shoes. Jack and Max ran to their usual escape route, but the ruffians were close behind and for all practical purposes the well-known curtains seemed about to descend on the handsome pair. Good fortune, however, accompanied them on this night. As they cleared the first fence and leaped down upon the concrete tennis courts, Jack and Max heard an agonized scream, the breath of it seemingly hot and heavy on their necks. They glanced quickly behind and saw the swiftest of the pursuers flapping crazily against the fence like a strange banner in a terrific wind storm. The pursuer dangled by one finger, his expensive, large stoned senior ring caught in a stray link of the metal wall. His cries startled the other pursuers into a temporary confusion, but Jack and Max were not so befuddled. They mounted the fence on the opposite side of the court, leaping almost halfway to their goal in a single bound. When they reached the top they paused, straddling the horizontal strut, and shouted: "You chickenshits" and "You're lucky you didn't catch us." Then they fled into the darkness, matching stride for stride and gradually stepping up the pace quite beyond the reach of any goddamned tennis player in the United States of America. Once across the Texas & Pacific tracks they slowed to a competitive trot and began laughing. They laughed all the way home through the darkened, sandy streets, many blocks of which they personally darkened.

Jack and Max recognized only one voice among the ruffians who had attempted to bully them. Revenge upon him was readily arranged. They searched for him in the schoolyard the following morning. When they located him—hanging around the snotty north side crowd that stood in a certain corner of the long portico twirling car keys around clean-nailed forefingers—they followed him to his locker. After making certain of the locker's location they prowled through the hallways until they found another locker with an unsecured combination lock on the door. Then they returned to the ruffian's locker, started a neat fire—using Bicycle Bob's methods—among the papers and other possessions in the bottom then closed the door, completing the task by snapping the borrowed combination lock in the handle. Their deed completed, Jack and Max retreated to the end of the hallway, sitting down on the hard composition floor to watch smoke waft gently from the slotted vents in the locker. They were disappointed by the absence of flame, but the ruffian's notebooks, lunch sack and tennis togs all burned steadily while the janitor banged away at the lock with a hammer, screwdriver and frantic breathing. When the door was finally opened, the damage was obviously extensive. One tennis shoe was still smoldering but the other shoe was almost completely destroyed. The lunch was reduced to a smoked banana and unidentifiable debris. Notebooks and papers were ashes and blackened fragments, recognizable only as treasures of sweat and valuable grades. "The son of a bitch should get some insurance," Max said, dusting off his Levis and walking toward his Spanish class. Jack strolled past the stunned locker owner, smiling, willing to forgive the stuck-up son of a bitch.

9

THROUGHOUT THEIR YEARS IN HIGH SCHOOL, the greatest influence upon Jack and Max was Dad Sterling, the legendary football coach whose teams seemed always to be involved in struggles for records and championships so important that accomplished veteran sportswriters were known to have burst into tears attempting to explain the desperation of the situation to amazed readers.

Dad Sterling was a large, fatherly-looking man whose head was covered by a fatherly-looking thatch of silvery hair. He had been so successful all of his assistant coaches imitated his moods and movements to explicitly they seemed to have thatches of silvery hair themselves; although the appearance was merely an optical illusion, a mirage of the mind rather than of the desert. These assistant coaches did most of the practical work on the practice field, but Dad Sterling always made his legendary presence felt. He would wander from group to group, pausing to advice first one young man then another in his resonant voice, a voice so mellow a famous columnist from Fort Worth declared his vocal chords may have been encased in walnut cabinetry. Dad Sterling did not believe in wasting his voice or his advice. As a result, most of his legendary remarks were brief, though not less prized.

"Don't let me catch you sneaking a drink of water, boys," he would say. "If I do, I'll kick the ass off of you."

Not drinking water was the only one of Dad Sterling's basic conditioning regulations and the only known violators were star halfbacks able to direct their paths to one of the mud puddles on the practice field where, after being tackled, they would lick dampness from the soggy earth while awed young boys from the neighborhood watched and dream of the day when they would be similarly tortured.

Jack and Max responded immediately to Dad Sterling and his silvery-haired ways. Max in particular was so enthusiastic he worked out on weight two or three times a day and soon resembled a hairless gorilla in his physical features. His biceps grew so strong and hard Max would walk with his arms dangling awkwardly—as though about to draw twin pistols—just to keep them from bumping his equally muscular rib cage. This was typical of Max, who considered full measures only half trying in any of his activities. Jack thought his own physique almost an ideal so was not nearly as zealous as his best friend. Even so, he would regularly accompany Max to the coaches' offices where Max liked to go whenever he had personal problems. The coaches would be sitting at their metal desks; their heads lowered while they drew diagrams of plays and formations, painted exhortatory signs, or made up Christmas lists from the sporting goods catalogues. Max always went directly to Dad Sterling and after he had finished telling the beloved coach his problem, the legendary figure invariably replied, "Don't bring that crap to me, son. I'm not running any kindergarten. If you want a sugar teat you should have enrolled in home economics"

The advice always appeared to delight Max, probably because each time he took a problem to his father, the father would talk for hours, first exhausting Max and the exhausting himself, although rarely discussing the specific subject or even remembering what the subject had been in the first place. This practice so irritated Max he confessed to Jack he had frequently resorted to prayer, pleading with God or anyone who would listen to provide his father with a liquor problem or anything else that would keep him from paying so much attention to his family.

Jack and Max played side-by-side through their years of high school football. Max's nose seemed to be constantly broken, but otherwise the most remarkable event of their careers came in the midst of their second year when the star quarterback resigned from the team, tearfully, because his parents—known to be religious fanatics—had determined football was a sin. According to close friends, they had arrived at the decision through prayer, a report that left the unanswered Max even more irritated.

Prowess on the football field paid off nicely in other respects. The most obvious one being admiration from the school's colony of females. Jack and Max solved their transportation problem by purchasing a rusting Model A and chopping off the top with a hatchet to create a convertible. They improvised a tail-light with an old flashlight and made similar modifications elsewhere. The end result required almost constant attention but, as usual, Max plunged into the activity with the fierce combination of his old fervor and his new muscularity. With their automobile and letter jackets—beautiful red coats featuring white leather sleeves and an enormous white chenille "O"—Jack and Max had no difficulty persuading female classmates to accompany them on convertible-riding adventures. If the girls had money, they would attend a drive-in movie. Otherwise, Jack or Max would motor directly to one of the cattle tanks where the couples would nestle above the prairie, sweetened breezes blowing into the convertible and herds of white-faced cattle nosing gently around them, squishing in the mud and slurping up the night-cooled water. Max would play his harmonica, Jack would sing melancholy songs, and the cattle would call out soft cattle calls under the West Texas stars, the most spectacular in the world except for certain parts of Nevada. The setting was so tender the girls frequently removed their fresh white panties and began unbuttoning their starched white blouses before Jack and Max could complete their song. This so vexed the talented pair may a young lady risked being struck squarely in the stomach.

For matinee romances, when they avoided classes, Jack and Max preferred to take their little sweethearts—those who would agree—to the city dumpground. The average garbage dump has an unsavory reputation but, like most things accepted in the proper frame, can be an engaging experience. Wandering around in the canyons of trash Jack and Max frequently stumbled across hard to find treasures—pieces of pipe, scraps of lumber and hardware, discarded auto parts—which they could adapt to their own use. Occasionally, on cloudy days, they organized rat safaris, stalking the wild creatures with home-made spears and their own native cunning. Here and there, old trash fires—still smoldering—caused clouds of smoke to drift about the canyons, creating an eerie world quite unlike anything else in the surrounding countryside. On some of these days Jack and Max wandered like tourists, strangers in an unkempt land. The smell was not pleasant, but smells rarely are, and if there were condescending people who held their noses and looked askance at dumpgrounds, those people did not include Jack Desbrough and Max Murphy.

While walking among these ruined ruins, Jack would consider his past, chagrined that it was not as bright as his future. Though he rarely knew where he was, he never felt lost, a recent discovery he realized was as important to him as the invention of fire was important to other members of the community.

Assisted by the dumpground's caretaker and the caretaker's retarded, drooling son, Jack and Max constructed—out of pipe and various other materials—an elaborate structure resembling the monkey bars found on public playgrounds and in the back-yards of wealthy industrialists. From this cobweb of pipe and rusty plating they attached hammocks, lanterns, a radio, a bat-tered weather vane, a canvas water bag, and an assortment of interchangeable novelties. There, suspended in space, the two companions spent many of their idle moments, making some of the moment idle when they might well have been otherwise—though not necessarily wisely—employed. On plates of sheet metal, placed in rows like United States government tombstones, they painted the important names, dates, mottoes, and numbers of their lives including separate lists of virgins they desired and would not spare and persons who had given them cheap shit. Some names appeared on both the lists.

Between the automobile and the iron cobweb their lives came quite close to idyllic. If you had asked Jack and Max they would have agreed it was so. They would have waited and wanted for nothing they did not have.

"To hell with Indiana," Jack said one afternoon, softly rubbing the sand from his blue eyes and concluding the search and yearn for that mythical green land. An awareness of "Self" had crept into Jack. A contentment. A knowledge that his life would be as good as he was. Jack continually met each day as quickly as it came and in the same order. In this manner his high school years passed quickly. He regretted having to learn so many useless things but realized he had otherwise extracted the maximum from his education while possibly contributing more than he had received.

There were no regrets when graduation week arrived. Jack had left almost nothing of importance undone. He was not one to carve initials in every niche, a device he considered only crudely effective considering the number of other people who might share the same initials. Nevertheless, he felt confident he had left a place for himself in the famous composition-floored hallways. Dad Sterling had called him the finest fumble recoverer he had ever coached, personally slapping him on the back rather than have one of his assistants perform the task. Wherever Jack walked, small children and some less-witted larger kids would flop over on their lawns and even on the sidewalk in front of the Lyric Theatre, imitating Jack's famous form embracing a loose football. At a tender age, Jack Desbrough had attained a measure of fame. Fortune would come later and so would other things too numerous to catalogue.

During the final senior class assembly—an incredibly sentimental occasion—Jack and Max were asked to sing and play for the last time. They followed the tearful farewell speeches and the final chorus of the alma mater with the saddest song in the world.

'Tie me to your apron strings again,
I know there's room for me upon your knee.
Bring back all those happy hours when
you kissed my tears away, from day to day.
I thought that I was right but I was wrong,
Please take me back tonight where I belong;
Sing those cradle songs to me and then
Won't you tie me to your apron strings again?'

Neither Jack nor Max was surprised when the song stirred the audience to hysteria. Indeed, Jack was most often surprised when he was not surrounded by hysteria. Even so, the two could not help being interested in subsequent events. Three girls rose spontaneously in their widely-separated sears, declaring they would remain students in the high school for the remainder of their lives. Even more dramatic was the complete breakdown of the grizzled old woodshop teacher who was often accused, perhaps unjustly, of loosening safety devices on his whirring equipment in order to watch as his startled young charges leaped back with splintered or near-splintered fingers.

Max wanted to leap from the stage and slap the crying girls, a tactic he had seen employed by famous movie stars called upon to subdue hysteria. Jack, however, convinced his best friend he should wait until the girls were less hysterical. "People who laugh when you get in a fight with a girl have never been hit by one. I have. A girl can hurt you."

Max, as he so often did, agreed entirely with Jack's famous logic. Too often, Jack had proved himself the master of a situation and if Max wanted any other example he had only to compare their respective football careers: Jack Desbrough with his collection of recovered fumbles, Max Murphy with his broken noses.

Jack had become, in this melancholy graduation day, a leader of men. Now he need only find the men.

10

BETWEEN THE FINAL DAY of high school and the first day of college, every young man who goes from one to the other is faced with a series of weeks, amounting in the end to approximately three months, during which he must prepare himself for this most serious exploration into serious scholarship. For some, the effort is comparatively simple and routine. Their fathers and grandfathers will have already assembled some form of wealth and they have only to remain alive and otherwise conscious to assure themselves of a lifetime of pleasure, big-game trophies, licked boots and genuine self-respect for a job well done.

For others, Jack Desbrough included, the task can be made considerably more difficult by the tyrannies—some tiny and some immense, some accidental and some imposed—associated with employment. There are only three positions worth having and those three are permanently filled. A few others offer some opportunity for advancement and financial reward, providing the young man is willing to mortgage the best years of his life and keep his nose and similar features clean.

Very little time or effort was required by Bicycle Bob, even in his feebling state, to explain these things to Jack and to convince Jack he was destined for a better life than that of the wage slave or employee. Jack did not believe his apprenticeship at the bicycle shop had prepared him for many of the usual occupations, but the wise lad had to agree he was too good for them even if it had.

Consequently, Jack was quite prepared to sit out the poignant summer listening to Bicycle Bob during the afternoons and to his weary comrades drifting homeward from their work on pipelines, drilling rigs and other hot metals during the evenings. For several hours each day, until the sun began seeping through the tin roof in the horizon over his head, Jack would consider his future. Whenever he drifted near discouragement—he never actually became discouraged—Jack would talk with Bicycle Bob. If his mentor's words were not encouragement enough, Jack had only to look at his tiring and aging friends to know he had made the correct decision. Even Max Murphy, who ordinarily enlisted immediately in all of Jack's plans and projects, fell into the employment dodge. Max unloaded bags of cement; heaving them onto his shoulder and carrying them from boxcars into trucks and from trucks into warehouses. Because of his muscles Max performed nearly every chore, even the purchase of postage stamps, stripped to the waist. On each working day he was covered--before noon-from head to food in gray cement dust. When Max trudged from the T&P tracks down South Lee Street to join Jack and Bicycle Bob, he resembled a marvelous, heroic statue freed from the mold and searching for a town square. The gray dust would drift in gentle puffs from his great body and a crowd of happy children and assorted dogs would trot along behind, shouting to envious contemporaries who were not permitted out of their front yards.

At first, Jack and Bicycle Bob reviewed this parade without comment although each, in his own way, was quite impressed. Admittedly not so impressed either ever felt the urge to unload cement. Gradually, however, the two of them grew uneasy around

Max's prosperity. From the casual friend and nephew they had known, he became the owner of a delicately-jeweled wristwatch with a gold mesh band; from the accomplished accomplice he was transformed into the possessor of a dainty bank book exactly like one treasured by an aging seamstress or a retired vocal coach.

Jack and Bob wanted to snatch him back but, true to his character, Max clung stubbornly to what he had begun. It was easy to see that in the same way he had built his muscles and hacked out the convertible he would now attack employment. One day he might put the bank book down but, if so, it would be only to begin on another.

"Guess you'll be buying a tennis racquet next," Jack blurted angrily one afternoon. Max blushed and denied the charge, but his protest was weak and unconvincing; and his toes wiggled guiltily, as though they were already encased in canvas shoes.

With regret at the good times past, Jack suggested to Bicycle Bob the day had come to cease waiting for Max every afternoon. Bicycle Bob readily agreed. The oddly-allied pair turned back to the domino parlors along Grant Avenue. They spent the entire day in those dark temples, so cool the atmosphere clamped on their bones like a mother's chill. Here, Bicycle Bob had taught Jack some of the lessons absorbed so long ago they seemed new again. Here, nothing was changed except chance and Bicycle Bob was so skillful at the domino games there was rarely any chance in that.

Had anyone measure the distance, they would have discovered the grandest of the shabby parlors to be located exactly between United States Highway 80 and the Texas and Pacific railroad tracks. Wanderers, including strange troubadours with instruments they could not play and songs they could not sing, would pass through on their route to the California gold fields, bartering and trading with the adventurers who had journeyed no further than their sturdy chairs around the felt-covered tables.

71

Sweat was instantly dried here, and good luck exchanged for cash. There was reason enough to leave the place, though not reason enough to go anywhere else.

Once, the unsuspecting Jack was talked into employment while he sat at the elbow of Bicycle Bob and sipped from the old man's can of beer. The talker was a flatterer, a knave who dripped names and hints of currency idly through his conversation, using them as casual punctuation: glittering items that floated back-and-forth and slowly hypnotized the dozing Jack.

The fast talker was a former crony of Bicycle Bob, a dandy little man with a half pint of Old Crow seemingly permanent in his hip pocket. He claimed to have played guitar in the finest clubs in New Orleans, to have sailed all but one of the several seas and to have shoveled manure at both the rodeo in Madison Square Garden and at the Fort Worth Fat Stock Show. By profession, he was now a wandering street decorator, a rare artist whose work appeared on principal thoroughfares at important times.

Between the two of them, Jack and the dandy little man spread a rainbow of color over some of the dullest—previously dullest—minor towns and communities in West Texas. They helped celebrate Rattlesnake Derbies, Fourths of July and Old Settlers' Reunions. With a few nails and red, white and blue bunting they cured eyesores and restored ailing national holidays. The job was a satisfying one and Jack might well have remained forever at his curious position atop ladders and among the oft-maligned tubes of neon few men ever really know or understand. Might have remained there, that is, except for waking up one morning and finding the dandy little man gone from the cabin they had shared in a sunburned, paint-peeling tourist court on the outskirts of Seagraves. The room was incredibly hot and quiet, empty except for Jack and the flies circling busily around sticky, opened cans of pork and beans and sliced pineapple on the bedside table. Jack dressed, slowly, and then walked into the depressing sunshine. There were no clouds and no indication there would ever be any clouds again. The dandy little man's old brown automobile and the orange trailer full of pleated red, white and blue decorations were gone. Jack realized immediately, even though he had not had the experience before, that he had been abandoned, stranded among strangers, without so much as a single paycheck to show for his weeks of employment. He replaced and retied his shoes, then sat upon the ground-level porch and leaned back against the screen door of his room. He resisted the impulse to feel sorry for himself and listened instead to the humming of the flies inside the room and the humming of the traffic, bound north and south, on the highway in front of the tourist court. Jack imagined he could hear the additional sounds of kitchen doors slamming and firearms being loaded, but he could not hear the sounds of the dandy little man returning. He stood and walked slowly to the highway, the town's principal avenue. Looking northward, Jack could see the result of his yesterday's work, hanging limply in the breezeless air. Looking southward, he could see the route home.

Jack crossed the highway and stood on the edge of the pavement, where the sidewalk would have been if there had been a sidewalk. Blotches of the asphalt were already softening in the patched areas. He was too proud to use his thumb to signal for a ride, but stood nonchalantly, thumbs hooked in his Levi pockets. He was picked up, almost immediately, by a young United States Marine, one with a single chevron on his sleeve.

For a few miles, the Marine explained to Jack how he had never taken any crap from any man or woman during his entire life and was not planning to begin now. Jack said he had never taken any crap from anyone either although occasionally it had been given to him. The young Marine said he did not like smart aleck remarks and sometimes considered them crap. Jack wanted the ride home as desperately as he had ever wanted anything and for that reason refrained from elaborating on the argument. Instead, he closed his eyes and lapsed into a study of revenge, day-dreaming of dynamite and other explosives, followed by a parade along boulevards he had decorated himself.

The United States Marine carried Jack to within a half block of Bicycle Bob's favorite domino parlor. Jack found the old man there, almost alone. Entirely alone at his table. Bicycle Bob said he was surprised Jack did not already know most of the trouble in the world was caused by feisty rascals like the dandy little man. Jack said he was surprised Bicycle Bob's advice always came after it was needed.

A Mexican sitting at the next table laughed at the spectacle of the old mentor and the young apprentice arguing between themselves. Jack and Bicycle Bob frowned at the Mexican, injuring his feelings considerably; or at least the Mexican always insisted his feeling were injured during subsequent recollections of the afternoon.

The Mexican leaped to his feet, angrily, and shouted, "You think I'm a Mexican, don't you?" Jack, who was rarely startled by anything, including shouting, could not instantly reply to the question. As a matter of fact, he did think the Mexican was a Mexican, but that was obviously not the proper response. "I'm Indian," the Mexican said, slamming his Mexican-looking fist across his chest. "I'm a full-blooded Indian as good as any man in this place."

The Mexican said he had an automobile in excellent running condition and offered to drive Bicycle Bob and Jack out into the country where he would whip the hell out of them, providing they would pay for half of the gasoline. Bicycle Bob said he had no particular craving for having hell whipped out of him and was not buying gasoline for crazy greasers even if he developed a craving. Jack did not think this was the thing to say, not out of fear of having to fight the Mexican so much as loathing for standing out in the dusty prairie and fighting under a sun undiluted by clouds for thousands of miles. He could imagine lying in the dirt, on his back, while grasshoppers and other jumping and crawling intruders slithered and leaped around his remains.

The Mexican did not seem to resent Bicycle Bob's calling him a greaser, presumably to reinforce his case for Indianhood. Instead, he sat down between Bicycle Bob and Jack and tipped his chair back on its rear legs so he could lean against the filthy wall. "Old man," the Mexican said, "We need old men like you in politics. This is the only town in Texas without any corruption in high places. You could fix that."

Jack believed the Mexican to be joking or insulting, but Bicycle Bob appeared to take his words seriously and soberly. Before long the Mexican had become serious himself. After two hours of intense conversation, Bicycle Bob announced he would be a candidate for Justice of the Peace of Precinct Four. Jack and the Mexican, who said his name was also Bob, would be his campaign committee. The Palace Dominoes was not in Precinct Four, but neither was any other decent accommodation, so they named the table they sat around as their campaign headquarters and Bicycle Bob ordered three bottles of Pearl, their campaign beer.

Elaborate plans were discussed and develop immediately. Bicycle Bob insisted he would conduct a bitter and intensive campaign aimed to get certain sons of bitches. Bob, the Mexican, agreed this was noble and necessary, but added there was no great hurry since no other candidate appeared likely to contest for the position and Precinct Four was notorious for slender pickings. The last Justice of the Peace had resigned in mid-term complaining he was plagued by chiselers who wanted a cut-rate on their wedding ceremonies, bullies who called and threatened to beat him up for sentencing their little brothers to ten days in jail for malicious mischief, and angry niggers seeking injunctions to keep the Mexicans out of their neighborhoods.

Bob, the Mexican, wanted to begin the campaign with a series of letters to the editor demanding paved streets, lighted thoroughfares, a few sidewalks and more Bermuda grass and swings for the South Side Park. Bicycle Bob, the candidate, was reluctant. "Nobody reads newspapers and nobody reads letters and double nobody reads letters in newspapers," he said. "What we're going to do is go out and meet the voters, show some interest. After we've started collecting fees, we can worry about good deeds. I'm running for justice of the peace office. Not for scoutmaster."

Jack, hoping Bicycle Bob was joking about serious campaigning, soon lost interest in the conversation. The time for enrolling in college was not far away and, with the taste of dread appearing in his beer, Jack realized his future was no better planned than his past. He had the sensation of being some sort of eccentric fruit which was all peeling. As the fruit pared away and pared away nothing was ever uncovered, no juicy morsel, not even a seed. He felt sick and walked into the alley to piss on the mound of discarded playing cards, his stream eroding a deuce of hearts. "I know this isn't the best I can do," Jack said aloud. He ignored two whores, leaning out of the hotel window across the alley, shouting "Sweetheart" and "Baby" at him and whistling, but he felt better. He felt like a sweetheart.

A week later Bicycle Bob walked into the Palace Dominoes carrying two boxes under one arm. Inside the boxes were pastel green, blue and pink cards announcing Bicycle Bob's candidacy for Justice of the Peace of Precinct Four, pledging honesty and integrity, and asking for votes and influence. Bob, the Mexican, wanted to give away something more substantial, an emery board or a packet of needles, and Bicycle Bob said he might do that during his first re-elections campaign, depending upon the fees he collected.

Max Murphy helped distribute some of the cards for his uncle but the bulk of the labor was assumed by Jack and Bob, the Mexican. They divided Precinct Four between themselves and set out to place Bicycle Bob's cards in every screen door on the South Side. There were no problems to this sort of campaigning beyond a few dogs who seemed to have been trained at some strange establishment specializing in the protection of the seedy and decrepit. Jack, by nature, was kindly disposed toward animals, but did not hesitate to kick hell out of any cur attempting to impede the planting of a card on the master's screen door.

Following each day's work, the campaigners returned to the Palace Dominoes to report to Bicycle Bob. Truthfully, all the reporting was done by Bob, the Mexican, since Jack never had anything of significance to contribute. According to Bob, the Mexican, his appointed routes were filled with housewives who appeared nude at their doorways to accept the cards. The naked women were mostly wives of doctors who usually invited him into their homes where they engaged Bob, the Mexican, in incredible sexual endeavors, some of which took him an hour or more to reconstruct. Jack could never understand what it was about Bob, the Mexican, to attract so many doctors' wives. For one thing, Bob, the Mexican, was ugly and mean-faced, as charming as a collection agent. For another, Jack had never heard of a doctor living on the South Side. Jack did understand that his own route was dull and desultory. Instead of naked housewives he encountered ill-tempered watchdogs and small children with filth flowing out of their noses and diapers and down their chins and skinny legs. Only once did he meet a housewife at a back-door. She thought he was some sort of Halloween prankster out on a summer holiday and threw a basin of soapy water on him.

The day he met the housewife who doused him with dishwater, Jack determined to abandon politics, but when he arrived at the Palace Dominoes he found Bicycle Bob and Bob, the

Mexican, looking so cheerful he told them instead that he had met a housewife who had dragged him into the shower with her, soaking his clothing. The news seemed to please Bicycle Bob and Bob, the Mexican, immensely. Jack suddenly realized he, too, had been meeting doctor's wives all along.

Shortly afterward, Jack and Max, Bicycle Bob and Bob, the Mexican, sat around the table, playing moon and listening to the election returns on the radio. There were infrequent reports on Precinct Four's Justice of the Peace contest, but those which came through made it obvious Bicycle Bob was going to fail. A schoolhouse janitor named A.C. Jackson, called Ace by the children in the first through sixth grades at South Elementary, was compiling an enormous advantage entirely on write-in votes he had not even solicited. The small group around the table grew quieter as the size of the defeat grew greater. Jack realized he could not care less about Bicycle Bob's embarrassment, but he saw no merit in the explanations of Bob, the Mexican, who said Ace Jackson was winning because the voters did not really know him. He suspected Bob, the Mexican, was not being as consoling as he sounded.

All that remained of the campaign were a number of Bicycle Bob's little cards. The old man took them out of a box and shuffled them, mixing the blues, greens and pinks in an extraordinary pattern on the green felt table. Tears sparkled in his old eyes and Jack, looking away into the people passing on the sidewalk outside, considered the heartbreak of the election count, the certification that you are unnecessary. He was glad the summer was over and hoped Bicycle Bob would not actually cry. Jack knew he would not cry himself, knew he would not waste another summer of his life by working and would never ask for approval.

11

THE YEARS OF YOUTH WERE FINALLY DONE
so far as Jack Desbrough could determine. He sat—on a gas
meter painted with thick layers of silvery paint—directly across
the street from his home, contemplating the monuments he was
leaving to other years and other eyes. The American Museum of
Natural Jack.

A stranger, passing, had there been such a stranger, would
have guessed Jack's preoccupation and walked on, quietly: on tip
to or other silent conveyance.

To this interested stranger, Jack's eyes would seem to have
been directed upon the house numbers, figures fading in the
early September twilight. The deduction would not have been
entirely awry because the numbers were certainly an investment
in Jack's sentimental nature. He had painted the numerals himself, as a childish gesture intended to please his sweet mother as
she hummed and danced in the kitchen. Jack had used a large
black crayon for the task. The effect, while crude, was not entirely
without charm. His mother had been pleased, as he had expected
her to be, and promised she would never move from the address.

Yet, despite the alignment of his eyes, Jack's attention was not
upon the numbers nor upon anything anyone could have seen.

He was looking far beyond the view, toward things he wanted to see rather than things to be seen.

Jack could reconstruct, for example, the curly slice of bacon that had fallen from the breakfast table onto the kitchen floor, lying there for days while the grease soaked slowly into a permanent pattern on the scarred, scraped linoleum. Not a sentimental verse, perhaps, for those with cradles stored in attics, souvenirs framed in carved wood and curved glass, preserved delicate Valentines, glittering costumes from celebrated masquerades; but Jack Desbrough could have wept for all the lost, lonely, greasy bacon in the world.

He did not weep. Almost no child of West Texas ever does in his lifetime, not through fear of emotion so much as the fear of the softly falling dust and the arrangement the mixture of tears and dirt make upon the cheek, an effect sparing neither the handsome nor the ugly and rendering ridiculous the most sentimental of moments. Imagine a dry, windy day in April, a funeral, a minister sober in sorrow, a new widow, a dust devil raising her skirts.

In reality, Jack had none of these thoughts. Instead, it occurred to him that of all the children of the land he was perhaps the one best prepared for the future.

Jack realized quite well that it was this future, not his past that was most important. He had already survived all the past there would ever be and the remainder of his perils lay away, probably in some geometrical pattern easily charted had he subscribed to the proper technical magazines or enlisted in the appropriate elective courses. Yet, it was the past Jack brooded upon, and if he could change things it was this he would have altered. Not the future.

A parade of memories, daydreams, mirages, recollections strode before him. Some hurrying to close a gap; some slowing for spirited exhibition, while others piled up behind them. Some passed twice and others, whose backs he could see disappearing over the horizon, had not gone by at all. Goosesteps, limps, stumbles, and childhood relays. Marches and hymns. Narrow escapes, close calls, skins of teeth. Rooster fights, board behinds, brags, bluffs, retreats, revenges. Lucky drawings, successful thefts, early risings. Bloody noses, mouths and elbows. Itchings and cravings.

Gradually, the noise of the windmill, twisting in the collected breeze, emerged beyond the music of the Nostalgic Woodwind Band. The Festival of Sentiment began to fade and Jack's reverie clicked from a mural of emotional fragments, rendered in the Mexican style, to sharply designated images, framed in modern metals and plastics.

If he had been directing the placement of neatly-lettered placards under the various exhibits in his Museum, Jack would have started with the row of pecan trees around his family's property. They were not really trees, having never grown from the slender, virtually leafless saplings they were when they were first planted, but each of them merited a notation, all of them together a still greater notation. In the sense of success the trees were an obvious failure; their stunted, awkward, scrawny posture producing neither shade nor fruit nor sanctuary from predatory beast. Yet they stood, still living, and Jack could see them as the one viable reflection of his existence. He doubted they would ever grow, but conceivably they would never die, having come this far.

There were eight of the trees in two rows forming a backward L. Frequently, during outbursts of competitive intensity, Jack and his friends in the neighborhood had raced around them, sometimes in furious sprint, more often in leisurely, boyish marathon. The trees had served as goal lines and boundaries, targets and markers. From the viewpoint of tree-loving and beauty they were an eyesore. From the viewpoint of Jack's position atop the gas meter they were a giant redwood forest of memory.

Beyond the trees, in front of his house, was the tiny lawn, no larger than a living room rug if his home had had a living room. Each blade of grass was surrounded by sand but—like the trees—endured, and, from a proper distance, appeared to thrive. Jack had wrestled his boyhood companions on the lawn, absorbing and enlarging certain skills of self-defense, many of them later deplored by Bicycle Bob, but all of them eminently sensible and usable at the time of the emergency. He would have preferred a softly-hilled, closely-clipped lawn draped with sunlight and decorated by quietly-pecking peacocks; but man rarely has the opportunity to choose his own grass.

From the wrestling lawn it was an easy crawl under his house and Jack had made that elusive journey many times. The slightly-stifled earth beneath, and the framework and flooring above, comprised a sheltered enclosure he was not likely to find again. Jack could recall virtually every instance he had crept into the shadowy hole. Most of them had been trifling errands to retrieve one or another of his dogs—the misfit, castoff, once one-eyed mongrels he possessed in an abundance approaching pack size.

Not all of the crawlings, however, had been in search of new puppies. Once, locked out of his home, Jack had lain on his stomach, his cheek on his crossed arms, through an entire summertime rainstorm, feeling safer than he had ever felt before. On another afternoon, the afternoon he had leaped from a neighbor's tool-shed rooftop and caught his nose on a clothes-line, Jack's home had been filled with his mother's friends and he had crept beneath the shelter to die while he listened to the sounds of girlish and the clink of coffee cups and spoons. Beneath the same floor, Jack had discovered things about himself—his mind and his person—he never forgot, never mentioned. He had hidden things there, some of them curious childish items he had outgrown between the hiding and the next recollection.

They would remain there, among the dog bones, forever: ruins without an archeologist.

Behind the house was the metal windmill, quietly clattering now, capable of superb whirlings, a tower of uncounted trials of endurance and courage: dodges among spinning blades, slides down the water-cooled pipe, hand-by-hand grappling over the perilous height from the derrick to the redwood storage tank. Around the windmill were played grave scenes of challenge and chicken, experiences that would shatter some childish nerves for the longer parts of a century; the creation of cowards, artificial and permanent, in an open-air, sandy laboratory. The wind blew through them all, breezes fanning their fevers as they weighed the impact of the dare never left unsaid. Everyone was a survivor, even those who died right there, beneath the sparrow's nests and the slowly-dripping water and the contempt of their companions.

Jack was leaving now, he knew, and though he had not told him mother, and never would tell her, he was not coming back, not even for Christmas or Thanksgiving or his own birthday. Youth can be used for only so long and Jack would not need his again.

* * *

A strolling child, flying a gigantic June bug on a leash of thin black thread, walked past Jack. The last of the sun glimmered on the silvery gas meter and the metallic green wings of the buzzing bug. "What're you doing, Jack?" the curious child asked.

"None of your damned business kid," Jack replied, pleasantly.

12

JACK'S DEPARTURE was not nearly as melancholy as he had planned and hoped the occasion would be. Although he could not claim sophistication in either travel or university life, Jack knew some gestures of farewell should be exchanged with his family and friends at the Texas and Pacific depot. His guess, based upon the example of motion pictures and similar observations of life, was that his mother should be at the station wiping tears, fruitlessly, from her eyes. Then his father would clasp him close to his chest and wish him good luck, not being able to say anything else for fear of revealing emotion. Finally, the turn, tender, of his best girlfriend would come, her own tears confusing her sweet cheeks and her fears for his departure eroding an ordinarily demure public manner.

Unfortunately, Jack did not have a father, his mother was much too busy, and he did not yet possess a genuine girlfriend. He would have been alone at the station except for the unexpected arrival of Bicycle Bob, who had heard of Jack's departure and appeared with the rumble of the west would Eagle already detectable along the trembling wooden platform where Jack stood with several large crates of oil field equipment. Arlene had wanted to accompany him, but Jack told the little bitch, again, that although she was his sweetheart he wanted her to keep the hell away from him. Arlene had complied, and for purposes of this narrative, disappears, save for one very brief appearance. Not dead, but never again needed.

Bicycle Bob had partially recovered from the loss of the tinsmith's wife and the devastating debacle of his political career. He had taken on the appearance of a mechanic who had fallen asleep under a chassis dripping with oil and grease: refreshed but dirty. Jack was not enthusiastic about his old mentor's presence, neither his person nor his place on the platform. He would have preferred his exit to be a lonely one, a dignified melancholy he could elaborate upon all the way to El Paso. Instead, Bicycle Bob stood around, his hands in his khaki trouser pockets, the breeze disturbing his thin old gray hair as he spoke cheerfully of Jack's growing up. "You won't be back this way, boy," Bicycle Bob said.

Jack had no response for this remark, considering that it was an accurate appraisal of his plans. Jack was running away to join the world and the last thing on his mind was returning home. This was the circus train, but he could do without the clowns. "Kiss my ass goodbye," he serenaded himself and whoever else listened in on his thoughts.

When the train arrived, brakes squealing and dust swirling, Jack clutched his single suitcase, shook Bicycle Bob's hand hastily and was inside the coach before Bicycle Bob had time to contribute any more of his famous advice. Jack had enough of that to last a lifetime.

He chose a seat on the side of the train opposite the platform so he would not have to wave goodbye to the old man. As he looked out the window and down South Lee Street he was startled to see Arlene standing in the middle of the sandy avenue, her hands on her hips, staring at the train. Jack did not think Arlene could see him, but in the event she could he slumped down in his seat and closed his eyes. He kept them closed until the train started with its reliable clanking and appeared to have gained maximum speed. When Jack next opened his eyes he was looking out upon the nearly empty prairie west of town. He was gone.

It seemed to Jack that if he had ever found a natural habitat that habitat was on the train. He wandered along the aisles of the cars, purchased sandwiches and soft drinks, sat in the observation saloon, peered out the window at the platforms, yellow depots, and idle freight cars in Monahans, Pecos, Van Horn, Sierra Blanca and the other casual stops and unnamed lurching between Odessa and El Paso. Curious cowboys in pickup trucks peered back at him at dark crossings; Mexicans, sitting idly among the crates of freight, looked back at him too and Jack wondered if they wondered where he was going. This was Travel and for the first time, in a very long time, Jack was pleased at his progress through life and life's reasonable facsimiles.

The nearly two hundred and fifty miles to El Paso passed by in an incredibly short time. Jack retrieved his suitcase, scarred but sturdy, like the young man himself, and walked through Union Station into the Border Air. He rejected suggestions of taxi rides from taxi drivers, not so much suspicious of their vested, albeit artificial, interest in his welfare as of his own uncertain destination. And or destiny.

As he strode the darkened streets, returning eastward toward the glow of downtown light, Jack passed two surly strangers lurking in an alleyway entrance, lighting cigarettes and muttering to themselves. One of the strangers looked up, wickedly, as Jack strolled past and asked Jack how much would he like his Texas ass whipped. Jack walked on. He could tell from their odd speech the strangers were Yankees, from California or New Jersey, and Yankees were known to be mean and angry men with no regard for human life or injured feelings. Jack wished them little harm beyond unmarked graves. Following Bicycle Bob's instructions, Jack did not befriend or otherwise mess with Yankees, diseased dogs, or knife-scarred women. No good, in the end, could come of a relationship with any of them.

Locating the YMCA was no problem. Jack was momentarily nonplussed by the grouchiness of the aged desk clerk in an atmosphere where he had anticipated only cheerfulness and healthy shouts, not unlike those he once expected to hear in his imagined life in Indiana. He was puzzled that an old man would be working in a Young Man's Christian Association, but it was not Jack's manner to question the vagaries of existence, even when that existence was likely to affect his own.

The room assigned to Jack was crumby but clean. Jack could live there, particularly since he was not likely to spend much time in a room. Some persons—individuals who mend socks and befriend insects—can learn a great deal about rooms by staying in them, but Jack never did this so his speech and thought were rarely seasoned with references to peeling wallpaper, ratty window shades or burn-scarred bedside tables. There would be enough of these in Jack's future but he made no effort to observe them, and he would have been surprised had an agent of the Relevant Government Bureau presented him with a statistical table demonstrating the shabbiness of his history.

Peace accompanied Jack's Spartan dreams—based for the most part—on his experiences in real life. The dreams were so realistic he could easily have substituted portions of them for his own biography. Past pains and pleasures were past whether genuine or merely inspired by disturbed sleep. Tomorrow morning, when he awoke, Jack would encounter the first of his days alone in reality as well as mind. Within twenty-four hours he was determined to be a man and, sadly for himself, he wished this last night otherwise to be as innocent as he, himself, was innocent. In this respect Jack's wish was granted. A warranty honored.

* * *

The morning, and Jack, were fresh when he stepped outside and walked down the steps into the sun and street. All of him—his body and hair and teeth—had received attention in the shower room. There was no cleaner person in the world, at this moment, than Jack Desbrough and he intended to change that.

Jack paused in the middle of the Plaza to review the alligators sunning themselves in their odd enclosure. These alligators were ageless beasts, stirred only rarely, and might easily have passed for dead. Over a period of months, Jack observed them almost daily and only twice did he detect a noteworthy movement beyond the swish of a powerful tail. It seemed to him the alligators were resting for an important day and Jack, in whimsical mood, would sometimes lounge on Plaza benches and speculate on what that occasion might be; some holocaust, some private urge or passion, some revolution of the captive or gathering of the reptiles. He could imagine any one or all of these events occurring. His speculations, however, were reserved for a later date than this one. On this First Day, Jack harbored no such thoughts. He was en route to grudges, narrow escapes, diseases and cures, everything that looked, smelled and tasted of life. Time to be lost and time to be spent. He was gone.

* * *

Following a noon-time breakfast of orange juice and corn flakes in the Hilton Hotel's drug store, Jack spent an hour leafing through magazines and two more hours in a large downtown movie theatre, watching a Technicolor feature which made him yearn to be a great jazz musician riding around the country in a bus with good old pals who told merry jokes and blew their instruments at pretty girls.

When he walked out of the theatre and into the sun, Jack decided the time had arrived for him to begin. Darkness was still three or four hours away, but Jack had set no boundaries on his ambitions and did not require either darkness or illumination for his plans. At a shooting gallery, he fired several rounds at puzzling but humorous replicas of beloved childhood figures. When he ceased firing, Jack knew he had not done well, but the proprietor of the establishment—a distinguished old gentleman wearing an Uncle Sam suit—presented him with a marksmanship medal. The medal was a six-pointed tin star hung from a ribbon of miscellaneous colors, reminding Jack of his father's World War I victory medal. Jack could see the thing itself was not particularly distinguished, but he preferred not to injure the old man's feelings and wore his new prize out into the gathering gloaming. He was not surprised at winning rewards for his efforts. Jack expected them. He would have accepted a less ostentatious reward even though little Mexican boys kept shining his boots and the lower portion of his trousers whenever they saw the bright star reflecting the glow of the neon lighting and its own ribbon. Three of the little boys insisted on following Jack on his route, then waited outside while he went into penny arcades to peer into the peepshow machines. A smart aleck, making change, said he had never seen a marksman on the premises before. The smart aleck became very quiet when he observed that Jack viewed him as no more than a large target bearing several pounds of nickels and dimes on his belt. The medal loomed as an even greater reward.

Jack enjoyed the peepshows. The girls were pretty and there were times he asked no more of them. He realized they were only clever imitations of the real thing so he stepped into the street again and began walking South. Toward the Border. The walk was a long one so, Jack occasionally stopped at taverns to drink cans of beer. He would have preferred to merely pause and sit on the sidewalk curb, but each time he attempted this, the shoeshine boys following him would spring upon to his boots. His trouser cuffs were beginning to be heavy with was and his feet were bothered. On one corner, across the avenue, he watched two young men beating and kicking another man. The activity was solemn and silent. The man being beaten and kicked reminded Jack of himself, but he knew it was someone else. He moved on.

Jack, finally, arrived at the International Bridge. Small boys—like those who followed him—stood on sandbars in the middle of the river below. These little boys waved paper cylinders mounted on long sticks and shouted appeals for tourists to throw money at them, then scrambled in the mud after the pennies. Jack was turning pleasant as the beer mellowed in his stomach. He smiled into the twilight and recalled amusing anecdotes concerning niggers who could spit like quarters. He regretted he had not developed this ability.

While he was looking at the boys on the sandbars, Jack's young companions had been busy at his boots again. Jack waved good-bye to them as he crossed into Mexico, smiling at their childish attempts to coax a tip from him. One of them cried that Jack was a chickenshit cabrón, but Jack did not even look back at the little dickens. He had never curried the favor of snot-nosed shoeshine boys and he did not presume to begin now.

"Marksmen don't put with nobody's crap," Jack said to a puzzled old lady who was pinning a sprig of flowers opposite his medal. He did not choose to play the fool and make the usual mistake of tourists so did not tip the old hag either, a non-action that seemed to anger the proprietor of a bull-whip and souvenir shop nearby. The man made a gesture of contempt which Jack

91

returned in kind as he continued his adventures into manhood in a foreign land. There were people who got up early enough to frighten Jack, but he did not expect to meet any of them on this date.

Jack was astonished at the number of virgins who resided in Juarez. Within two blocks of the bridge at least six taxi drivers promised to introduce him to one of them, an offer Jack took no more seriously than he would have an attractive offer for his soul. He had no yearning for virgins: "They're about as useful as a Republican justice of the peace," Bicycle Bob would have said. Had said.

At the insistence of several doormen, Jack was soon enjoying himself in nightclubs and bars, drinking whiskies and beer and greasy liquerish offerings in small glasses. He was somewhat surprised at the ease with which he made friends among the women in those places although not so naïve as to believe everything they said about his curly hair and healthy teeth. Twice, Jack was smitten by one of his new friends and was induced into spending a part of his pleasure on them. Both the ladies were delightfully pretty, dark-haired and gold-toothed. Jack would not have minded remaining under the downy quilts for a greater length of time, but on each occasion the same grandmotherly looking old woman came to the doorway and told him to get his Texas ass out of the bed or she would summon a particular personality from down the dismal and dark hallway. Jack was not certain who the personality was, but the old woman indicated he was a fantastic brute, related to the president of Mexico, who would not hesitate to use either violence or political influence to achieve his ends. Although Jack was not frightened and even suspected the personality might well be a quaint and colorful little old man hovering furtively in the background, he could see nothing but trouble resulting from tardiness and so pulled on his glistening boots and departed. He was beginning to weary, but so was the evening, and when the evening was gone, Jack was determined to be there still.

At one bar Jack paused to listen to a marimba band play "The Poet and Peasant Overture" and at another he paused to eat a steak sandwich and listen to a customer, standing with one booted foot on his chair, sing popular songs to his sweetheart or at least to the woman he was serenading. Jack thought the singer was a trifle theatric, but would not have minded having a beautiful companion or a manly baritone voice or both. While he was listening to the singer, Jack fell into conversation with two young Mexican men. One of them claimed to be a radio star from Monterey and the other made no claims at all. The two proposed that Jack join them in a contest to see if they could drink a different drink in every bar in Juarez. There would be no winner in the contest, but the first to fall unconscious would be left by his companions to die or be dragged away by constables.

"Only losers here, Charley," one of the men said, mispronouncing Jack's name.

Because Jack found his new companions to be entertaining fellows, the contest was a pleasant one for him. He knew they expected him to be the first to fall, but he did not expect to be so he did not worry about that. He sampled drinks he had never heard of before and in three bars—when the customers heard of the contest in progress—he did not even have to purchase his own drinks. In one bar, Jack discovered that he did have a romantic baritone voice after all and he and his new friends sang "Mexicali Rose" and "It Happened in Old Monterey" and other Gene Autry selections. The three of them ignored the whores and winos who booed and shouted and tried to drown out the sentimental music.

Tears crept into Jack's eyes, though he would never spill them, when the Man Who Had Made No Claims passed out and fell into a pile of salt he had carefully prepared to consume with a

93

bottle of tequila. Jack and the Radio Star left him lying there in the midst of whores patting his pockets.

Dawn was coming up like thunder in Jack's head as he and the Radio Star reached an intersection, arms clasped around one another's shoulders. Without a word they parted and went on their ways, the Radio Star to unnamed places, Jack Desbrough to the International Bridge.

Jack vomited on each side of the border but in the middle of the bridge he stopped and looked down at the little boys with their poles and paper receptacles. Solemnly, he ripped the sprig of flowers from one shoulder and tossed the bright bouquet down to the children. Then he unpinned the marksmanship medal and threw the shiny six-fingered star into the glow of the sunrise.

Men do not need medals to know when they are men.

13

IN THE LIFE OF MOST YOUNG MEN, and Jack had now proven himself a man, there is a time for learning. Even in a life crowded with advice, prescriptions, encyclopedias, high school and similar apparatus. At least Jack Desbrough assumed there would be some learning attached to his university years.

Admittedly, he was enrolling principally to enjoy the comradeship of the men in the dormitory, to sit around log fires sipping spiced drinks on long winter afternoons while snow piled peacefully on the window panes. In other seasons, there would be strolls across lawns strewn with affluence of giant trees and there would be much hailing of bright-cheeked co-eds and contemporary scholars. There would be pauses to discuss the events of ancient days with professors whose tiny beards and large eyeglasses were the insignia of their great learning.

Jack did not fault his campus for being located amidst the rocks and sands of the desert. He would rarely see snow, he knew, but it took a great deal more than excellent weather to discourage Jack Desbrough.

As soon as he reviewed the list of subversive organizations he had never belonged to and signed his non-Communist affidavit, Jack was admitted to the bursar's office and permitted to make arrangements for paying his fees. He was not chagrined by these rigorous requirements. A university education was not for everyone and Jack had not expected things to be easy. Indeed, would have been disappointed had they been easy.

Jack wished to be considered bright and he was more and more viewing himself as a traveler en route to Yukons and Patagonias, preferring this profession to those that involved bilking the public. (Although he no longer harbored peculiar illusions about the public's need to be bilked). Consequently, he wished to quote poetry—not too much poetry though—and to otherwise appear wise to those he encountered in his travels. He was not averse to learning the peculiarities of business arithmetic and to speaking in an Italian tongue so he enlisted in those courses as well as in the various literary lectures.

Jack was assigned a dormitory room with a wizened young man who wore thick glasses and a decorative complexion of various colors. The young man introduced himself to Jack as X.L. Whisenhunt from Dallas Texas. He asked Jack if Jack was from Laredo. He seemed disappointed that Jack was from Odessa and this made Jack disappointed too. Jack imagined X.L. Whisenhunt felt about Laredo the way he once felt about Indiana and Jack, kindly Jack, did not like to see every human being's feelings tampered with. He volunteered to retire and permit X.L. Whisenhunt to resume his search for a Laredo friend, but X.L. rejected the proposal. "There's no use," he said, obviously hurt, "Everybody wants a roommate from Laredo and the frat rats get all the first choices."

Jack was surprised at this reference to a beloved college tradition like fraternities and doubted the accuracy of the statement. He, for one, had never heard of anything special about Laredo, discounting certain hot weather reports.

X.L. was not Jack's idea (certainly not ideal) of a college roommate but, as usual, Jack had no fears about fitting him into his scheme. In addition to his interesting complexion, X.L. Whisenhunt possessed an enormous collection of country and western records that he played loudly at all times. He also kept a supply of dynamite under his bed, which he used to startle the campus at regular intervals. Also loudly. X.L. promised to kill Jack if Jack ever revealed anything about either the records or the dynamite. All in all, Jack was rather disappointed in his new companion even though he was aware X.L. would have to become one of his great friends, joining Buck Jones Hickey and Max Murphy on a slender list. It had long been Jack's belief that a man should like his best friends and he could barely tolerate X.L. Whisenhunt, who also promised to kill Jack if he joined a fraternity or attempted to piss on his (X.L.'s) bed. Jack had experience in one of the items but had not actually planned to do either, even though X.L.'s apparent hatred of both created new yearnings in Jack's breast.

Anyone could sense X.L. Whisenhunt was near insane, perhaps entirely insane, and Jack would have preferred a more conventional roommate, perhaps a blonde fellow who wore horn-rimmed glasses, smoked a pipe and was, hopefully, a campus leader. He told himself he had nothing against rooming with a maniac—Jack prided himself on his tolerance and nonchalance—but wished someone else had been accorded the privilege.

X.L. Whisenhunt claimed to have burned down two fraternity houses and to have shop-lifted every single one of his hundreds of C&W records. Jack had no reason to doubt either of the boasts, but did not think either was particularly noteworthy; although, to please X.L., he did not say this.

Eventually, Jack and X.L. were to become great friends and would share many collegiate adventures together. X.L. remained insane, but his hates and rages began to make sense to Jack and X.L. accepted Jack as his equal, even giving Jack one of his handsome, pearl handled revolvers, explaining that he had three and could manipulate only two at any one time. Since X.L. had trained himself in strange talents like writing upside down, Jack professed surprise that he could not handle three handguns, but accepted the gift gratefully.

Despite his periodic threats to kill Jack, X.L. was basically a kindly person and actually made life easier for the both of them.

They devised and developed an excellent system for the football season. Jack had to make certain personal sacrifices to arrive at the stadium early enough to obtain a seat on the topmost row. From there, he could watch the game and also keep an alert lookout for X.L. as he roamed the parking lot below busily rifling automobiles for profitable items like whiskey, blankets, picnic baskets, radios, barbecue sandwiches and other loot that could be exchanged for currency in the dormitory. Jack was not a criminal by nature and always asked X.L. to take only the things he needed more than the owners, the same system he had worked with Max Murphy. X.L. paid no heed to this request and always finished the evening's work with a number of odd products like baby strollers and patent medicines for female disorders.

"Laredo, I know what I'm doing," X.L. would say whenever Jack protested the useless risk involved in stealing so many profitless objects. Obviously, X.L. did not know what he was doing, but Jack—now called Laredo by his roommate—accepted his explanation rather than fruitlessly argue.

On two occasions, X.L. even invited Jack to accompany him up the side of one of the mountains near the campus, where he set off dynamite charges to "wake up the frat rats." Jack assumed the blasts, some of them thunderous, also woke up everyone else on campus because they frequently shattered windows and produce small avalanches. The university's authorities seemed to accept these explosions as part of the school's existence. They were never reported in newspaper accounts or condemned in bulletin-board lectures. X.L. had set off so many they no longer even caused a discussion in the cafeteria breakfast line. The students were a little sleepier but, if anything, they seemed proud to be a part of a university harboring a mad bomber.

X.L.'s worst enemy was a skinny freshman who called himself Big Chief, explaining that he was thing but tough like the famous contraceptive device. Big Chief sometimes lurked among the overhead pipes in the shower room, pouncing on people who had slighted or otherwise offended him, and attempting to beat the hell out of them. In this, he was not always successful, although he was so persistent he frequently managed to extract apologies from people much stronger than he was, a feat he wasted no time in boasting about. His claim to being the greatest nuisance on campus was a constant irritation to X.L., particularly on the occasions when Big Chief insisted he was the school bomber.

The rivalry between X.L. and Big Chief was a ludicrous one and, all too often, involved Jack in schemes beyond the range of his good humor. He saw nothing really funny about coating the sleeping Big Chief's shoes in rubber cement and then setting the mess on fire. Nor could he entirely appreciate the hosings, water gunnings and assorted wet activities that frequently accelerated into all-night conflicts involving complicated timing and the skidding of huge blocks of ice, large enough to bowl over a human target and, conceivably, break furniture and legs.

Jack supposed these were the famous college pranks and tried to enter into them whole-heartedly, but as the casualties mounted and the rivalry between X.L. and Big Chief gained grim resemblance to the dangers of tong wars, his interest waned.

Consequently, Jack was not entirely displeased the afternoon a senior, Steve Hatfield, called him aside and asked if he could speak to him about his associations. Steve Hatfield was very near the ideal Jack had in mind for a roommate. He was blonde, wore black horn-rimmed glasses, possessed a manly physique only vaguely covered by his lumberjack shirts, and spoke in a husky, authoritative voice.

"Jack," Steve began, "I've been watching you and I think you have all the qualities we look for in a university man. We were thinking you might enjoy life and this school a lot more if you didn't hang around X.L. and those other crazy guys so much. Maybe you ought to think about some things for a while and then we'll talk about your moving into our house."

Jack was immensely pleased by this attention from one of the campus coolies. He was also, however, instantly alert to the tones of do-goodism and the hint of fraternity life, anathemas inherited from years of Bicycle Bob's advice and X.L. Whisenhunt's scorn and threats. Jack was certain rooming with a lunatic was better than rooming with fraternity men and he resolved that he would not fall into the well-known snare of manufactured friendship and good cheer. He could use Steve Hatfield, but Steve Hatfield would find he could not use Jack Desbrough. He would find this out very well.

* * *

During succeeding weeks, Steve Hatfield introduced Jack to a side of life previously existing only in his thoughts. It was exactly like the side of life he had yearned for so long ago during so many quiet moments. Steve took Jack to quaint campus drinking establishments where students whiled away the hours of their youth singing and waving giant steins of beer, icy fragments sliding slowly down the sides of the steins. The two new friends strolled the campus together, calling to Steve's friends, male and female. Some of the females were striking women whose looks reminded Jack of famous magazine cover and abandoned day dreams. Jack and Steve attended pep rallies and musicales together, pausing afterward to chat with even more of Steve's friends, of whom there was an apparently endless number. Jack was dazzled by the collegiate life and how perfectly this life seemed to suit him, forgetting—as so many heroic figures seem to do—that all of existence fits neatly around the shoulders of those it favors: Jack should not have been surprised at all.

Despite the dazzle, Jack was not entirely satisfied with his new environment. He was somewhat uneasy about X.L. Whisenhunt, who did not say anything about Jack's new friends, but contented himself with speculative looks at Jack as he bent to his evening's work, either polishing his revolvers or cataloguing his new records. X.L. was using Jack, as Jack was using Steve, and this knowledge curdled in Jack's thoughts. He did not mind being used, since the using had been quite profitable; but X.L.'s recent schemes continued to be directed not so much at profit as at humiliating Big Chief.

The climax of these events came one evening after X.L. had lured Big Chief into the huge garbage incinerator and pumped .22 caliber bullets into the metal contrivance, causing the bullets to ricochet around his terrified rival and, in turn, causing the Chief to scream and plead for pity and assistance. Like most of the others in the dormitory, Jack was reluctant to interfere in the rivalry, but he did seize upon the occasion to pack his meager belongings and walk quietly out the front door into the darkness, tired of all college life but less at war than at peace with his emotions.

* * *

Jack remained in Steve's fraternity house for a few days, but wearied of the routine almost as soon as he began it. This particular house favored the crackling fire he had been expecting, but the fires were induced by imitation logs fanned by air conditioners in several windows. The atmosphere was pleasant enough, but the conversation was less so. When the frat men tired of talking about their fraternity they changed the subject and talked about other fraternities, including Jack in their speculations even though he was an outsider rumored to be hiding from the campus bomber, a rumor so false Jack never bothered issuing a denial. A few days of listening to the boring fraternity men made Jack yearn for his maniacal friends and he half hoped X.L. was looking for him and would add this house to his list of arsoned structures.

Dreams are too often realities. One night, Jack and the fraternity men were roused from their beds by the smell of burning fraternity house. Most of the young men, including Jack, escaped from the blaze. They were wearing their assorted collegiate sleeping clothing as they stood outside amidst the yucca and cactus plants and listened to the muffle, anxious shouts of those still trapped inside. Jack suggested the brothers should try and rescue their friends, but the suggestion was dismissed by the fraternity men, some of them even snickering at his naiveté.

"My father pays good taxes for the fire department," one of them explained, not unkindly but with a trace of condescension. "Let the goddamn firemen do the goddamn rescuing."

Jack walked away from the scene and back to his room in the dormitory. He suspected the air conditioning breeze fanning the false logs had fed the fire, but there was always a chance X.L. had set the thing off. Jack found his old roommate sitting on the bed, inserting blasting caps and fuses into his dynamite, tapping his metal-toed shoes and singing "San Antonio Rose."

"...Moon in all your splendor..." X.L. sang along.

"X.L., tell me the truth. Did you set any fires tonight?" Jack asked, smiling.

"Laredo, I'll tell you the truth," X.L. answered.

102

The two old friends, reunited, clasped one another in a fond, manly embrace, X.L.'s sooty fingers, hands, and arms making a strange X on the back of Jack's sweatshirt.

14

ONLY RARELY IN HIS LIFETIME had Jack had an occasion to employ his remarkable charm. The presence he sought for himself was peace of mind in a serene setting and this seeking did not require many displays of magnetism. Little more than a faint smile or a shrug of his shoulders was necessary, and Jack employed these to ward off everything from X.L. Wisenhunt's maniacal outbursts to veiled threats from his professors. Some of these men and women expressed puzzlement at Jack's peculiar study habits and infrequent classroom appearances. Jack, as is remarked, had not enrolled in the university to spend the better years of his young manhood mired in classroom rhetoric. His body and mind were a sanctuary and he could think of no reason to desecrate either with false idols or false ideals.

Knew of no reason, that is, until he met Belle Delgado, half-Mexican beauty, the beloved of the university, the most desirable young woman Jack had ever seen. Belle was tall and had long black hair she controlled with a snowy white headband worn in a Grecian style. She possessed powerful, graceful legs and breasts and a clean, clear mind unmolested by cruel or crude thoughts. She favored parasols to avoid over-freckling, and spent much of her time in cool, darkened libraries, reading to herself on the rare occasions she was not accompanied by a retinue of admirers, of whom Jack was the most recent. By tradition, Belle was the beloved possession of Steve Hatfield, whose status as the sharpest man on campus entitled him to numerous awards and honors, the company of Belle Delgado included.

Despite Steve Hatfield's popularity and overtures toward friendship, Jack early concluded he could stomach the man. Many of us question the motives of decent, well-meaning people, realizing that all hypocrisy originates in their being, so Jack cannot be faulted for this especially after he had seen Belle Delgado and realized only Steve Hatfield stood between him and sentimental attachment.

Belle assumed Jack was attracted to her. All men were. But the difference in this instance was that she was also fond of Jack. He was so entirely different from Steve Hatfield, and his All-American ways, his class offices and extra-curricular honors, his athletic achievements and headlines in all-capital letters, his ambitions and scholastic standing. She saw no reason why she should not have both Steve and Jack. This was not so much selfishness on her part as exactly the opposite. Belle knew there was enough of her to go around.

As clandestinely as possible—Belle's face and figure were known for miles in every direction, even south of the Border as far as Chihuahua City—she and Jack began seeing one another. At first, their meetings were quiet and unobtrusive, small gestures of trust and conversation as they grew more comfortable in the other's company. Jack sat with Belle in a darkened theatre balcony, his hands clammy with perspirations while she stroked his fingers and peered with squinted eyes—her one weakness, but a pleasant one—at the distant motion picture screen and its Italian characters. Later, Jack sat with her under the shade trees of the Plaza, watching his favorite alligators while he explained his theories of suspended evolution as the creatures bided their time awaiting a second turn at roaming the earth. Belle listened as she licked a vanilla ice cream cone. A recent raid by X.L. Whisenhunt and some friends, who inserted the large reptiles into various classrooms and professor's offices, had reduced the alligator population; but enough of the alligators remained to inspire speculation.

On another evening, Jack took Belle to a holiday festivity in Juarez where wild cowboys and would-be cowboys in bop glasses jumped upon the stage, fending off desperate security personnel, to rip articles of clothing from first startled and then tearful strippers. In the midst of this bedlam, Belle sipped as calmly at her crème de menthe as she had at her ice cream cones.

Finally, the conflict with Steve Hatfield now a reality, and Jack began escorting Belle to campus attractions. The difference being that Steve took her inside and Jack kept her outside, sitting under the flagpole during the nights of autumn, holding her in X.L.'s tattered convertible, with the top intact, during the nights of winter. (Jack frequently slept in the same car; as the room shared by X.L. and himself was now smelling acridly of alligator mischief).

It was on one of these winter evenings that Jack first topped Belle Delgado, tasting that sweetest of all punches and leaping in the trap from which one never escapes. Nothing he had done with Arlene, nothing he had sampled with his Juarez sweethearts had prepared Jack for the moment so many anticipate and so few realize.

There was great rain and thunder for the performance, the sort of storm and weather that arrested Belle's attention. The two of them were sitting in a parking lot, alone outside a crowded basketball arena. Belle had relaxed from the preliminary kissing and had begun reciting the ten most beautiful words in the English language, an exercise she preferred to Jack's poetry because the poetry contained so many words that were not beautiful even though they might lead to beautiful thoughts. She repeated special favorites—"dawn" and "hush" and "melody"—while Jack instinctively unbuttoned her soft cashmeres and imported woolens.

Light from the arc of the street lamp flowed into the battered convertible, reflecting into a misty glow all around them. Rain drops, sliding down the windshield, made ghostly, dark running shadows on the automobile upholstery, each drop resembling a tiny, frightened demon scurrying back to Hell.

Belle, sometimes influenced by her inferiors, had been attempting to learn to smoke and started now to push in the dashboard lighter to ignite a cigarette plucked delicately from a scented holder.

"You shouldn't smoke," Jack told her. "You're the prettiest girl I've ever known and it looks like hell for you to smoke. You're one of the prettiest girls in town. A half million guys think the same thing. They'd beg for a chance to be where I am."

"I won't do it again," Belle said, grateful for the advice. "You're so good for me," she sighed as Jack stroked her belly.

"I sure like you ass," he replied in his courtly manner.

"Jack, I think I may be a one-man girl after all," Belle said.

"That's me," Jack replied. "One man."

"I went to bed with Steve once. That wasn't right do you think? What should I do?"

"Talk to the man upstairs," Jack said quietly, his left hand reaching resolutely beneath her skirt for the lace over lace covering.

Jack was captured now, a prisoner of maximum lust. He stalked Belle Delgado in crowds and in solitude; his stoic coolness disturbed whenever she took an evening to continue her permanent romance with Steve Hatfield, a romance she assured Jack would eventually lead to an ideal marriage, doubly ideal since she intended to include Jack in her plans and to live as happily ever after as she was living now. Belle, in her sweet way, saw everything right in her reasoning. Though she was, as she said, a one-man woman, she still required two men.

Jack reduced his bare classroom appearances even further in order to be near Belle, who rarely had to go to class herself—so eager were her professors to be of service. The two of them, Jack and Belle, sat many afternoons in the Plaza sunshine, Belle reading aloud to Jack and to curious bums who gathered around pretending interest in literature; some of them lying supine on the walkways hoping for a glimpse up Belle's skirts. Many of the bums showed off and bragged outrageously, dancing or singing or playing jazz on a harmonica or talking trashily before the dark beauty. Jack would have preferred that Belle take up with one of these ragged, talented vagabonds rather than continue her relationship with Steve Hatfield and his clean-cut, do-good ways. Almost daily, Belle had to explain that a healthy, happy husband was necessary for a successful marriage and Steve was the only healthy, happy person she had ever met. Jack reluctantly agreed this was so and his natural fairness made the fairness of the argument apparent.

Jack did not ever propose marriage for himself. Not even the thought of having Belle Delgado forever would change the singular course he had outlined, a course that would take him to obscure trading posts in Alaska and Asia, to mountain bazaars and concerts featuring undiscovered orchestras. He would need no companions, no compasses, and no complications. He realized that life was much too short to be enjoyed all the time.

Nonetheless, Jack could not tolerate the thought of Belle being possessed by another man, particularly one so decent and wholesome. One day, Jack wandered—no by chance—into the university library. There, he saw Belle Delgado and Steve Hatfield sharing a book and a table and laughing quietly together. They looked splendid and happy, but Jack only vaguely noticed Steve Hatfield. His eyes were entirely on Belle, clean and fresh and seemingly untouched by human gropings. She sat at the library table, skirt above her knees, legs smooth and then even smoother before his eyes. She was a desirable prize, a trophy for having defeated this life, and Jack temporarily desired her above even his own ambitions. He could have blinked away tears, had tears appeared, but instead contended himself with squaring his handsome jaw and gritting his healthy teeth. Jack saw nothing amusing in their amusement and he turned in his tracks and marched back into the sunshine. He was halfway down the front steps when he heard footsteps and unmistakable voice of Steve Hatfield behind him.

"Jack, Jack, wait up," Steve called and Jack waited, tight-lipped with disgust at himself for doing so. The last thing he wanted was conversation and Steve Hatfield. Jack's rival was not likely to permit any human being to pass without some form of recognition, so frightened was he of appearing to be a conceited ass.

"Jack, why didn't you come over and join us?" Steve asked. Steve Hatfield, of course did not believe the gossip that Belle and Jack were carrying on before and behind him. "Sometimes I think we're not really friends," Steve continued. Steve Hatfield did not actually think anyone could dislike a genuinely friendly person like himself.

"I've been waiting to talk to you," Steve continued. "I've heard you aren't doing so well in school. I can't get you a better room away from that crazy X.L. because it's going to take years for our fraternity to rebuild the house, but if it'd do any good I could arrange with my Dad to give you a loan or something and you could find a little better place. Maybe if you had the right atmosphere to study in…"

"Hatfield," Jack said defiantly. "Your two cents worth isn't worth two cents."

Steve Hatfield was startled by this remark, although not half so startled as he was when Jack smashed him in the mouth.

110

The two fought furiously on the library lawn while windows were raised and a large crowd collected, aroused from their carrels and the overdue desk.

Jack struggled desperately, aware that time and training were on Steve Hatfield's side. He thought of comic strip dialect and sound effects, the whoppity whops of his childhood. There was no real conclusion to the fight itself. A frightened librarian courageously hurled herself between the two contestants, barely escaping being knocked senseless onto the parched grass.

Steve said he had no hard feelings and was considerably puzzled to see that Jack obviously did have them. Steve regarded the disappearing figure of Jack Desbrough as he walked resolutely away. Perhaps he might have felt somewhat flattered, even pleased, had he known of Jack's old resolve, true to Bicycle Bob's advice, never to fight cowards.

Jack asked X.L. to refrain from dynamiting any of Steve Hatfield's property. He preferred to handle this conflict himself and realized he was already branded as the only man on campus who could dislike Steve Hatfield. He did not bother explaining Belle Delgado to X.L. because he knew X.L.'s opinion of all females was disparaging, excepting certain country music singers.

"You can't change the truth without lyin'," X.L. said. He was fondling and sniffing a wad of cotton from an aspiring bottle as though the cotton was steeped in a wonderful fluid. There's something else on your mind, not just a fight with Steve Hatfield. Maybe there's a girl involved. I've heard guys fighting over woman before. They were crazy and they loved grief. Tennessee Tucker sings a great old song about one of them. He fought over a woman and wound up with a dead dog and waiting for the electric chair. You've never heard a song sadder than that one. That song makes 'Old Shep' sound like 'Jingle Bells.' You want to hear it?"

Jack did not want to hear the song and he also did not want to hear X.L. Whisenhunt talk about his record collection. There may be duller people in this life than a man's friends, but not many.

Instead, Jack wandered down the street toward the bus stop. He was disconsolate. Drunken students, hauled back from the Border on various contrivances, staggered past, waving souvenirs of bull rings and stag movies and shouting for Jack to return to the dormitory and the real drinking. Jack ignored the call for the fun. He did not expect to have fun again. He squared his shoulders and walked on, past the bus and up the hill and down the hill to the middle of town, back to his roots with the Plaza alligators. As usual, the alligators did not move, although soldiers from Fort Bliss tossed cigarettes and twigs at them and called them creepy names. Jack hated the soldiers and admired the stoicism of the alligators, contented animals which could not be disturbed by anything short of kidnapping by X.L. Whisenhunt. Then their strong tails cracked furniture, smashed beloved museum-quality pottery and accomplished miscellaneous destruction. Bulls were supposed to die the bravest deaths and Jack fancied them in his musings, but he expected the alligators would not put on much of a show either. They were bulls with short legs, not likely to lose their nonchalant regard for a woman any more than they would for cigarette-tossing soldiers.

As he sat on the bench, watching his scenes, Jack realized he was nowhere near the serenity of the alligators although, like them, he was far from home and tormented by wandering strangers. He sat for several hours, permitting his long day to draw deeply into night before he started for the hill and the dismal walk back to the campus. His college days were over, he had determined that much. He was virtually finished in the classroom anyhow, casualty of formulas and phrases and laws of reason he had no reason to obey. He was Gone.

There was only the unfinished business of Belle Delgado and Jack would finish that right away.

* * *

Midnight had passed when Jack crept up the vine-covered rear wall of the women's dormitory. He was enveloped in an inky, providential darkness, but fever lighted his way and guided his hands and neatly-socked feet past the second floor and up to Belle's third-floor quarters. He rapped on the window and Belle, at first frightened and then merely surprised, allowed him into her room. She was wearing her nightgown, plain and simple but exotic over her grand body. Jack felt, at once the surge of excitement he always felt in her presence.

"Belle," he said in a whisper. "I'm going. I don't know where, but I do know when and that's now. I want you to go with me."

"Jack," Belle said, pleading. "I don't want you to go and if you do I don't want to go with you. You can stay here and I'll take care of you the way I've always done."

"That's over," Jack replied. "I'm gone."

"Jack, I'm not gone. Everything, everywhere is beautiful, but here is where I'm beautiful. I'm not gone. You know what I like. I like to be warm on cold days and I don't like cold days. That's all you're offering me. The least I can get from you is trouble. I don't want to see you again. You're not good for me anymore."

"Not good for you?" Jack questioned then answered himself, "I'll buy you a box of vitamins."

Before this dialogue could be resolved, Belle's door was flung nosily open and the house mother stood there, framed in the light of the hallway, her cold, gray, suspicious eyes prying over

Jack's indignant physique, her resolute righteousness collected for an explosion.

"Young man," she said to Jack, "don't you move an inch. I know who you are and you're in trouble."

Jack, cornered, wished he could trade his clenched fists for a revolver; perhaps the one X.L. Whisenhunt had given him so many weeks ago.

"Goddamn you, ma'am," he said, pointing a finger directly at her quivering heart and breast. He yearned for bullets of some precious metal and sighed for the once-more leadness of reality.

The house mother slumped down in a faint. Jack extended the middle finger of his left hand in a last salute to Belle Delgado and then he departed—ruined but proud—through the hall and down the main stairway. Naked, brassiered and otherwise clad and unclad young women cheered the rare appearance, but Jack paid them no heed. He was, once again, gone.

Several minutes later, Jack stood on a scarred hill, amidst weeds and debris of abandoned construction. His position was particularly ugly. But from it, he had a lovely view: the campus, with the whirling red lights of police cars near the women's dormitory; the dormitory itself, with its brightly-lighted windows, each window containing its bright co-ed. There was a haze and a softness in either his eyes or the scene below him.

Once more, just as he stood in Goldsmith looking at the horizon of burning slush, and just as he sat on a gas meter and marveled at his address, Jack was unafraid. Directly in line with his right shoulder the sun would be bearing down upon the East. Soon he would be able to see.

15

JACK THOUGHT OF THE OLD HYMN, "Do Not Be Discouraged," as he trudged between the rusting railroad tracks, hot in the springtime sun. Certainly Jack was not discouraged. His present world had arrived at a conclusion, but there is only brief mourning for endings—long despair is saved for continuings—and he knew there would be many other worlds, not the least nor the last of them the one along these narrow, silent, now tranquil Southern Pacific tracks.

Jack was aware he must depart El Paso, preferably in haste, and leaving was precisely the reason he was here. As an alternative there was the highway, where truck drivers mounted on enormous rigs were known to offer a young man a ride. He had not, however, considered the highway. Once, Jack had found his home on a train leading away from home and he proposed to resume the noisy wandering, limited to a border of iron bound in one defined and definite direction or another. Jack loved trains and the simplicity of their existence. They would go and he would go with them, either East or West depending on the trains and not depending on anything else.

He was a wanderer now, just as he had planned to be for a long time. He would not soon be seen in these parts or in any other parts. A man who needs no one certainly needs no place.

The first train, or at least the first creeping train, was heading west and Jack vaulted himself into the doorway of an empty box car. Discarded, crushed cardboard cartons were lying on the floor and he managed comfortable quarters for himself by piling several of the cartons in one corner. He had heard of hobos in his lifetime, but Jack did not consider himself a hobo and would have been chagrined had he been hailed as one by passing friend or stranger or hobo. Other travelers with unknown destinations recognize this feeling.

Jack sat in the doorway of the slow-moving box car, admiring the things he was leaving behind, though not admiring them so much he would ever miss them. Belle Delgado, the sweetheart of his life, was already receding, slightly, from memory; so was X.L. Whisenhunt, his insane roommate; so, too, was his brief college year. Now he faced real life, without musical accompaniment, and real life permits only swift memories and short encounters. Life is to be lived, not pondered.

As the train rumbled into a faster pace, it moved from Texas into New Mexico, crossing the faded desert with assorted rattlings and roarings, crossing with Jack blinking his eyes in the puffs of dust, licking his lips as he considered the thirst he had prepared for with a single quart jar of water snug in his suitcase. He ate one of his candy bars and drank a portion of the water, then lay himself down on his cardboard castle, alternately sleeping and staring wide awake as trestles and stops and miles were passed and left behind. To consume the time, Jack used his small pocket knife to carve figures and initials adapted from his life onto the box car walls and, later, onto the cardboard bed: curious etchings few strangers would ever see and none would attempt to interpret.

116

At last, at night, Jack chose a nondescript depot as his destination. He jumped from the train, balancing his suitcase with himself as he landed. He did not look at the name attached to the station's door, realizing addresses are of slight importance and are frequently altered. An Indian, working at a baggage cart, was the only person to see Jack alight and the Indian, who had seen people before, took no interest in the community's new citizen. There are people who are welcome into a city with baskets of fruit and coupons from dry goods merchants, and there are some who are not.

Jack revised the neatness of his appearance in the foul, reeking gentleman's restroom, weaving his image around the cracked mirror until he was sufficiently reassured. He absorbed the advice—"Be good to people there is so many of them and only one of you"—printed in wavering letters on the wall. Then he walked from the stations toward the main street of the small town. Bright lights attracted him and as Jack approached the lights he could hear sounds that similarly captured his attention. Neon sizzled and hummed and hints of the music of the day flowed in a harmonious throb from various doorways, alternatively morose and lively. By sheer good fortune, Jack had wandered into the town's honky-tonk district. This luck would continue during the next few hours as he fell in with bad companions who promised to show him all of America worth seeing. Jack would doubt the premise, but respected their ambition and agreed he would not mind viewing the Grand Canyon and unusual taverns on the beaches of California.

His new friends, Joseph and Albert, were hustlers who worked the tables, boards and alleys of the land, achieving their livelihood in the traditional American way. Only by finding the local champion and defeating him on his home ground could they extract their profit from the economic system. They were purists who did not chisel or otherwise waste their time with the poor

117

and deprived, preferring to leave that enterprise to the banks, loan companies and mortgage firms. In their quest, the two of them had been unusually successful and in their successes had become kindly, compassionate men not averse to sharing good times and sordid companions with handsome strangers. Jack was only one of a series of promising young men they had befriended and set loose on the countryside, wiser, oftentimes richer, for the experience.

Jack was making a supper of Wolf Brand Chili and a bottle of beer when he met his future companions. They were calmly and efficiently winning several hundred dollars from a syndicate of local players, destroying their opponents' concentration with witty conversation and needling remarks as much as with their own craft and skills.

Jack alternately, idly, watched the competition, as well as a young woman at a nearby table who was stroking the thigh of one man even as she passionately kissed another. Jack admired the way the woman distributed her favors. He was equally fascinated by the enormous profit accumulated by the two hustlers.

Gradually, Jack began talking to Joseph and Albert, the three of them sharing the common bond of strangers in a new town. By the time the games were over, Jack had agreed to accompany them on their Western travels.

"You only live once and that's too often," Albert toasted as they drove north toward Albuquerque. They alternated drivers at hundred miles intervals, the stops dependent mostly upon the availability of cold beer in well-capped bottles. Coyote hides were stretched on barbed-wire fences and everywhere were other signs of wild life and wild death. There were aging Burma Shave signs to read but many were missing one posting or another so much of the rhyme scheming was nonsense as though T.S. Eliot had yielded to commercial blandishment.

Jack, lying in the back seat, was reminded of the old trips with Bicycle Bob and Max Murphy; those days of his youth now so far away he could never get there again. Music was a constant in the automobile, Albert altering radio stations the moment a tune ended and the announcer appeared near comment. Even when he seemed to be dozing, not even listening,. Albert's finger would punch a button and the music would continue, uninterrupted by harsh news broadcasts or appeals on behalf of commerce. During the drive, the young allies listened to Mexican music and gospel singing, but mostly they listened to country and Western stations, this being both the country and the West. At intervals, Jack dozed off, grateful for the music and the beer and the feeling of contentment that filled his mind and body with the fuels and sounds of life.

The last time Jack awoke, the three of them were on the outskirts of Albuquerque, Joseph and Albert searching eagerly among the electric signs and other landmarks for one of the listings in their address book. They had minimal difficulty locating the Peacock Lounge, set back from the highway and surrounded by DeSotos, Fords and Chevrolets, scattered in the aimless fashion of carefree Americans on the hard-packed earth of the parking area.

"I'm mean when I'm sober," Albert shouted as they opened the door and stepped from the darkness of the evening into the darkness of the lounge. A slight cheer arose from one table and a lady, dubious lady, ran to Albert and clasped him in her arms.

"Albert Breed, where've you been? There's money in this town never been spent."

Albert and Joseph immediately proceeded to their business. Telephone calls were made and the room began to fill with men, some quiet and some loud, all attracted by the appearance of the famed hustlers, apparently coming to Albuquerque to claim money, property, prestige and women. The locals could have

119

saved all four by remaining at home or by refusing to answer the telephone calls, but the challenge was too great from them to resist and they swallowed the bait eagerly, knowing all the while that it was poisoned.

Joseph, the best of the players, stumbled around the shuffle-board table with a gin bottle in his hand. Jack suspected Joseph might be handicapped by the beer he had consumed, but he had, himself, watched Joseph fill the gin bottle with tap water. He knew no altering of the senses was likely to flow from that source no matter how many times Joseph swigged from its contents and despite the near-prayerful expectations of the alert and hopeful crowd.

After a few hours, Jack tired of watching his new companions collect their passage money from a succession of challengers, each one more intense, each one more unfortunate that the last. There was grumbling among some of the losers, particularly those who were thin skinned and aggravated by Joseph's and Albert's insulting remarks about their lack of skill. When the competition seemed to lag, Joseph would play blind-folded or take his turn using a broomstick, but the stunt only delayed—never stayed—the inevitable conclusion.

At first, Jack was welcomed as a friend of the champions. But the champions were too good, and nowhere is excellence long appreciated. Jack could feel a tenseness creeping about the lounge. He noticed it first in the attentions of a large bully who seemed to resent Jack's courtly treatment of his girlfriend, particularly when Jack stroked her round little bottom and, as they danced around the light and sound of the juke box, kissed her tiny pierced ears.

Jack had never appreciated the virtues of loud bullies and he was not pleased by the interference of this one.

"Don't mess with my woman," the bully protested.

Jack noticed the anger in the man's tone and felt his dislike surging into his thoughts.

"Leave him alone Red," the woman said. "He's not doing anything."

"I'll leave him alone as soon as I knock his ass off of his shoulders you silly bitch," Red shouted, barely politely.

"Don't call me silly," the woman protested.

Red sneered.

The sneer and the slur apparently incensed the woman, who stubbed out her cigarette on the side of Red's nose, raising an instant blister and creating a first-aid curiosity that ordinarily would have fascinated Jack. The woman stalked from the lounge, pausing only to light another cigarette before plunging angrily into the night.

Red, enraged all the more, snatched a beer bottle from Jack's hand and shattered the bottle over his own head. Blood and beer and shards of ice dripped down his nose and cheeks, "You're tough, but I'm tough too. Let's fight."

Jack sensed trouble. He would have preferred to settle affairs with his bare fists, in the clean-cut way, but he was not stupid so he reached for a heavy glass ashtray and a heavier chair and the fight began. Immediately, Joseph and Albert and assorted locals—the locals agile now that they had been relieved of their heavy currency—became involved. Shouts went up and good men went down. The Peacock Lounge was thrust into dim shadows by the frightened proprietor, who stood on the bar attempting to whistle and shout "The Star Spangled Banner." In the gloom, Jack, Joseph and Albert burst through the door and ran to their automobile. A few minutes later they were speeding out of Albuquerque, driving west into the ebony and purple horizon, the great West of Route Sixty Six. Souvenir stands, stuffed buffalo, traffic courts, carved and decorated mountains, and illustrated motels. The cooled evening breeze blew in upon Jack, again in the back seat, as he fingered his bloody lips and Joseph and Albert laughed and laughed.

Many miles outside Albuquerque, they stopped the automobile and slept. Jack was amazed at the comfort built into the Buick's upholstery and at the exotic dreams he could cultivate by dozing with his arms above his head. His mother appeared in some of the dreams and Jack appeared in all of them.

During the next day, the three companions watched the sun display the colors of the Painted Desert, strolled among the marvelous rocks of the Petrified Forest, and stood on the brink of the Grand Canyon. In the dead of the night they drove past the Great Dam and when they slept again they were in a motel room in Las Vegas, last of a remarkable day's natural wonders.

When Jack awoke early the next afternoon, Joseph and Albert were gone and Jack, momentarily, assumed he had been stranded again, surprised at how Las Vegas could seem so much like Seagraves. Then he saw a note, written on the motel's yellowing stationary and attached to the mirror. The note was signed by Albert. The words hinted of mischief and told Jack to relax until they returned with more wealth.

Unfortunately, the plan did not work as well as the note writing. When Joseph and Albert stumbled back into the room they were poor men, pale as any poverty, cross and vowing they would never set foot in Nevada again except for expeditions into arson and similar revenges.

"Those dealers were trash," Joseph said sadly. "You got to have trash so you'll know what's good, but there wasn't any reason for those cards to do that way." Albert reminded Joseph that playing cards had never been his specialty and that he would have crushed any of the dealers at his own games, but Joseph remained downcast, unable to become interested even as they crossed Death Valley. Heat enveloped the interior of the automobile and forced the three of them to strip to their underwear for the final miles into California.

They entered the well-known state sweating and sleepy, but Joseph's depression dissolved the moment they rolled upon California pavement. Although the countryside seemed ratty and dry, as dry as West Texas, Jack could feel the pounding of the Pacific beyond the Sierras. Like Joseph and Albert, he achieved a quickness of his impulses and his other pulse. The air smelled of miracles and clouds on the horizon formed arches and tunnels, an unmistakable invitation.

Joseph and Albert were enthusiastic about the prospects of renewing old prosperity.

"You never get a bad check in California," Joseph declared.

"And they've got bars with carpets so thick you just walk around bare-footed," Albert added, banging the steering wheel and honking the horn.

Jack dozed off as the list of attractions grew longer, wondering of California. He awakened when Albert abruptly wheeled the vehicle into a palm-shaded roadside parking area. They emerged from amidst the hot metal to drink milkshakes mixed with dates. "A sure sign," said Joseph, "we're in California."

Soon afterward, they were adrift among the freeways surrounding Los Angeles, cheering as they passed famous signboards and exits. Women who looked like internationally known movie actresses, riding in strange and exotic automobiles, drove along adjoining lanes, contributing their share to the traffic and Jack's exuberance. He thought it odd that none of the celebrated beauties looked his way, but Jack was far too proud to shout or otherwise call attention to himself. He felt a kind of pity for the movie stars and others like them who would never know him. He regretted Albert's moon shots, directed at the beauties, not so much out of fear of arrest or contempt of females as the indignity of riding in the rear seat of a vehicle with bare buttocks extending from one window.

Joseph and Albert knew California well and remained eager to teach Jack how to play the state.

Jack could see from their expressions of delight that he was in the midst of something near wonderful and often wondered why he could not enjoy pleasure as much as his friends did. Nothing could daunt or dim their ardor. From a dim distant hill, they exclaimed at how the famous cloud of noxious fumes and smoke obscured much that was ugly and indelicate in the city. They would have subscribed to Frank O'Hara's contention that the stabbings contributed to population control, but they did not read poetry.

They were cheerful in traffic jams, claiming they would establish records for endurance; and they loved to wander along the squalid street lined with ruining men and young women wearing bad shoes. They chummed with the depraved and the deprived, encouraged street-corner evangelists with cash and cheerful confessions of their own sins, some of them bordering on the embarrassing. They patronized seldom-advertised stores and little-known and shoddy products. No amusement was too minor to attract their attention. As a matter of fact, they were bored by world premières, major sporting attractions and long parades.

True to their word, Joseph and Albert collected their share of the moveable wealth, occasionally breaking long-standing pinball machine records or gaining praise for skill on lighted links. Executives, hearing of their activities, invited them to participate in croquet tournaments and the natural athletes soon added to their resources in that fashion. All this good fortune they shared with their good friend, Jack Desbrough.

At first, the three partners lived in a motel patronized almost entirely by basketball teams. The surroundings were comfortable

124

and the beds huge—nearly eight feet long—but they soon tired of hearing tall men bouncing balls down the hallway and sought more permanent quarters. They found them in a boarding house operated by a chubby, sensual widow who kept her gray eyes on them and left underwear drying in several rooms, more lingerie than she could possibly have worn.

Jack was charmed by the widow's habits and encouraged them. He had not had a genuine home in a long time so the attentions of the widow were welcome. He liked having her urge him to eat lettuce. She would not permit him to walk to the library or the newsstand without carrying sandwiches in a paper bag, the sandwiches wrapped in wax paper decorated with pictures clipped from magazines and stamps removed from her late husband's large and valuable collection. There were days, otherwise unmarked, when Jack could have sold his lunch for enough money to board a TWA flight to a French restaurant in an obscure province; but he, of course, did not realize this and even if he had the thought of having his sandwiches evaluated would have seemed ludicrous to him.

Frequently, the widow would include a mash note in the lunch, usually wrapping the message around the pastries and cookies she enclosed in the paper bag. Most of the notes were ribald and suggestive, causing Jack to blush when he unwrapped the food. Occasional acquaintances thought it odd that he was embarrassed by chocolate éclairs, but reasoned they were in California.

Fortunately for Jack, the cookies never promised more than the widow was agreeable to providing. Although she continued to leave freshly-rinsed underwear around the house, Jack concluded that laundry must be her hobby because she never seemed to be wearing underwear when he encountered her, whether she was troweling in her tiny garden or writing letters explaining neighborhood affairs to subscribers of the *Los Angeles Times*.

125

The widow rarely read newspapers herself, but believed others did.

Gradually, the widow claimed the position formerly occupied by Joseph and Albert, who were tiring of California and thinking of Alaska. They asked Jack to accompany them, but he explained they were merely the best friends he could ever hope to have in his lifetime while the widow was female. Joseph and Albert acknowledged the fragility of their claim and—when they departed—wished Jack good luck and warned him not to do anything they might do. Jack told them he had never met any Alaskans before and warned them they would have difficulty loading dice with frozen fingers.

Joseph and Albert drove away, waiving, and Jack felt a loneliness for them, but eased the sentiment from his throat by concentrating on his new domestic status. The widow had gentle ways and prodded Jack into accepting some of them for his own. He ceased biting his fingernails and began shaping them into streamlined, contemporary sets, one indistinguishable from the next. He curried the approval of the neighborhood by dressing neatly and polishing his shoes, tricks he had learned in the first grade but actually abandoned during the trek through rudeness, childhood diseases, stalactites and stalagmites.

On Saturday mornings, Jack would wash the widow's Mercury coupe, lavishing extra suds on the chrome and various technologies on the bird droppings deposited there as nature's amusing imitation of chrome. During holidays, even relatively obscure ones celebrating near-traitorous conduct, Jack and the widow displayed a huge flag from a staff mounted on the edge of the porch roof. Neighbors began to invite them to participate in bridge tournaments and suggested that Jack select a religion and a profession so they could place him in the proper civic clubs and private swimming pools. Jack understood their interest and for that reason hesitated to explain to them that his good citizenship was entirely intended to endear himself to the widow. He enjoyed eating his evening meal with her after the four other boarders, all retired school teachers, had returned to their rooms. The teachers hated the widow's hasty cooking and frequently wrote sharp reprimands, in red pencil, on their napkins. Jack, however, liked the food and never complained, even when he was served the same dish of beans and tacos night after night. He would sit at one end of the long table and the widow at the other end. Between them would be a plain of white cloth interrupted by a small crystal mountain, a candelabra with lighted candles that produced flickering apparitions of beans and Mexican food on the faded wallpaper.

Outside there would be echoes of shattered glass, cries of wounded children, a medley of squealing tires and distant sirens, shouts of dismay and anger; but inside the candle glowed serenely and the widow sipped at her glass of water, scenes Jack would not have exchanged for the treasures of Wall Street or Coney Island.

For the time he was content and realized he would be unhappy and dissatisfied when he departed, reasons that seemed quite good enough to him.

16

TRUTHFULLY, JACK WAS NOT PREPARED for the widow's reaction when he informed her he was leaving to join his friends in Alaska. Letters from Joseph and Albert boasted of masculine adventures as well as intimations that Jack could not stand up to the rigors of spring, not to mention any of the other seasons. Although he did not feel called upon to prove himself or even challenge his endurance, Jack did miss the comradeship of Joseph and Albert and could see no harm, especially to himself, in visiting them.

His life had become so pleasant and genteel Jack could almost hear Bicycle Bob, his old mentor, chuckling, whenever he unlocked the gate to undertake yet another trivial errand for the widow; tasks he knew would be rewarded with lavish displays of affection: platters stacked with freshly-baked cookies followed by new arrangements of the widow herself. If he did not break this habit of contentment, Jack realized he would be frozen in a still-life not unlike the framed reproductions the widow had installed throughout her boarding house. His postures of defiance would become no more effective than those of mean-mouthed fish glues to a polished hardwood plaque and mounted above a fireplace... Perhaps even a false fireplace.

Jack was quite aware that the widow liked him, but he did not realize she liked him so much she was prepared to damage his person for suggesting he might depart, however briefly. Her cries of outrage aroused the retired school teachers. One of them assumed the atomic holocaust for which she had so long prepared her little students was at last at hand. The tiny old lady became quite angry when she discovered her mistake and threatened extravagant use of the widow's utilities.

All this female noise left Jack uneasy. He wanted only to flee the premises and make his way north. The scheme seemed no more complicated than an extended shopping trip or another errand for Jack, but the widow insisted it would lead to heart-break for herself and unimagined hardship for him. Both were strong arguments, and in the event he needed additional evidence, the widow began to decorate Jack's breakfast trays with newspaper articles neatly pasted on heavy paper— some laminated—describing caribou herds driven into frenzied stampede by clouds of mosquitoes, trappers drowned in icy currents and then devoured by gigantic crabs, predictions of pitiless Russian amphibious assaults on neighboring islands.

The idea of Alaska paled almost as quickly as it had flamed in Jack's thoughts, now a poor third to the Dream of Indiana and the Reality of California. Even so, wanderlust had entered his bloodstream, thickening the fluid as thoroughly as all the other lusts. Jack realized he was not likely to ever enjoy a situation as pleasant as his current one, so he made an attempt at restoring peace of mind, laboring to develop a taste for literature, motion pictures, quiet music and even loveable pets.

None of these provided the solace Jack sought. His thoughts remained filled with holes and rough edges, more like a poorly-paved street than a well-ordered mind. He read avidly from a list of books reputed to have changed the world, but when he had completed the list he felt unchanged except that he was weary of printed words and subject to intimations of eye strain.

The bleakness of his literary venture channeled Jack into the motion picture theaters. After weeks of black letters on white paper, he developed a craving for illustrated life. For a very brief time he enjoyed his new surroundings, being not only twenty degrees cooler, but established in a tranquil environment patrolled by competent ushers in neat uniforms who refused to put up with any crap from noisy old ladies, and serviced by a concessions counter full of nationally advertised confections. Only the constant display of flickering entertainment kept sitting in the movie theaters from being an entirely pleasant experience.

Jack grew to resent the intrusion of filmed conflict, romance, and comedy into his otherwise peaceful afternoons. He could not understand the peculiar outlook of either the movie makers or the moviegoers. A sharply-kicked shin or a perilous predicament were frequently considered hilarious while long kisses and romantic dialogue were treated as a serious and painful business. This reversal of the obvious order did not so much puzzle Jack as disconcert him.

Adding to his discouragement was the scene outside the theaters where Jack could feel, see and smell the rubble of his time. Street lamps glowed in unmatched colors, recent fashions were unfashionable, telephones rarely rang in the booths he passed, sky writers placed false rumors among the rain clouds. Things were not adding up to sums that Jack liked. He despaired at his surroundings and surrounders, pale imitations of Technicolor without the benefit of an editing process that would leave the crass, the ugly, and the trivial on the cutting room floor.

Jack began to fear the remainder of his life would consist of a peculiar California boarding house, wherein he would be the hero of a melodrama in which nothing ever happened. The widow and the retired school teachers sensed his discontent and labored to amuse him. Jack was grateful for their efforts, but the teachers' offers to improve his Latin and handwriting were hardly worth the gesture of rejection; and the widow's favors were becoming so commonplace as to contribute toward rather than to relieve his tedium. Jack spoke less often now, dressed simpler, and excused himself whenever one of the teachers seemed intent upon conversation. Eventually, he was driven to the cheapest of opiates: he began to sleep through the afternoons, interrupting his naps to accommodate random dreams.

Jack's dreams, perhaps inspired by his recent disinterest in motion pictures, began to appear in a double-feature fashion; a rare bargain considering their rationing in his previous slumbers.

The first of Jack's illusions described his presence in a huge convention hall in a famous resort city, where great speakers, orators with thrilling voices, announced to the crowd that there was no more. When he awakened, Jack could not remember what it was there was no more of, but he did remember that all of the crowd, the great throng, was composed of himself, an international convention of Jack Desbrough. He realized the speaker was delivering a message for him and regretted he could never recall what the message had been.

The second of his dreams was more realistic—albeit a slap-stick realism—populated by characters and personalities all too recognizable from his own life and headlines. The dream began with the widow receiving a birthday check from maiden aunts in Nevada, old ladies so refined they rarely gambled before sundown and then limited themselves to quiet games with softly-shuffled cards. To celebrate the gift, the widow presented Jack with one half of the check's worth and suggested he employ the money to entertain "his best girl friend." Jack considered the blunt hint an outright dare, but in support of tranquility, invited the widow to accompany him.

Jack, of course, did not believe in corsages, diamonds, tattoos, or other false and peculiar decorations, but the widow embraced almost all of them. She wore a necklace, jangling bracelets, an ankle chain, earrings, jeweled eyeglasses, a diamond-studded tiara, a wrist watch, several huge rings and a gold-mesh belt. Jack assumed she had some ornament—a not untypical gesture of the widow—mounted into her veiled abdomen. He declared they would attract the attention of every deranged prospector on the West Coast and insisted the widow divest herself of a portion of her minerals, a request the widow resisted with cross shouts and declarations of personal freedom.

Jack could see the only way to win the argument was to call upon his Golden Gloves training. He considered this course of action, then, decided to return to his usual good nature. For one thing, he reasoned that once the widow was off her guard he could strip a few of the more garish pieces of jewelry from her dress and throw them into the nearest irretrievable. He was not one to bear a grudge with revenge was so easily at hand.

As it happened, the widow's costume was precisely correct for the Green and Goldenrod Café. The Café was inside an enormous building; originally a dirigible hangar, restored to its 1934 glamour and located on the estate of one of Hollywood's failed motion picture magnates. Contained inside the vast building was a sampling of California life Jack had frequently imagined for himself. "No wonder I never found it," he said silently, "it's been in here all the time."

Movie magnates who had not failed were dining in ornate, gilded boxes, each one serviced by an individual spot light. False clouds floated above the crowd and by knowledgeable manipulation of certain dials and coordinates the management could induce a tropical rainstorm to attack unruly patrons or ill-dressed tourists.

Famous Western stars, mounted on swift and equally-famous cow ponies, waited in the same serving line with young starlets. Most of the latter were alternately fainting or crying hysterically between glances at the disinterested executives. Jack was familiar with the old technique of bursting into song in public places. He had seen that performance in Juarez many times. But at the Green and Goldenrod, entire orchestras would rise to their feet and play sparkling rhythms, fandangos that set dancing waiters to tapping out marvelous codes. A huge scoreboard apparatus announced important entrances and departures, as well as birth and deaths and other noteworthy events almost as the happened. Many of the announcements were greeted with bursts of applause while the magnates and their entourages tossed down crisp leaves of fresh lettuce, hard candy wrapped in crackling cellophane wrappers, and replicas of famous coins of the past. This was life on a grand scale and Jack was not reluctant to enjoy it so long as he could keep his distance.

Like the regulars, Jack soon learned to remain in the middle of the room, out of range of the magnates' boxes and removed from the more active events like bicycle sprints, the watermelon festivals, and the conventions of mortgage bankers, munitions merchants and similar types specializing in joy buzzer hand-shakes and other practical jokes and mischief on man and womankind.

Jack was accepted in this atmosphere and the realization of his acceptance had the effect of springing him awake as though one of the conventioneers had introduced a joy buzzer into his bed clothing.

Once awakened, Jack realized he would ordinarily struggle to remain aloof from activities of this sort, although feeling a certain resentment toward the occasions when the activities were aloof from him. He marked the days of his dreams on a calendar in his room in the boarding house, promising himself that similar days and dreams would not actually appear in his life.

During the few weeks following his awareness, Jack prepared for his flight from the widow. Since he had only sentimental and affectionate feelings toward the woman, he saw no reason to injure those feelings by repeating his earlier mistake of telling her he was leaving. She would know that certainly enough when he was gone.

To obtain operating capital, Jack determined to contribute a pint of his valuable and available blood toward the future emergencies of unidentified strangers.

A familiarity with the backwaters and badlands of the city had been one of the several rewards of Jack's random ventures with Joseph and Albert. He knew exactly where to present himself, joining the line of men he had formerly observed with only casual interest.

The blood bank was near the flophouse and cheap beer district, but still within the range of the tour busses, one of which passed every hour, eager passengers peering out of the windows, yearning to identify a fallen celebrity slinking about the stench and decay. Famous old villains and silent screen roués were rumored to frequent the place, having achieved their just deserts.

The line in the reception hall of the blood bank was long, but curled in a tight rectangle all the way around the room, the last position backed up to the registration window where the first arrivals were standing. Jack could identify none of the people ahead of him in the proceedings, but had never placed any faith in the celebrity theory anyhow. He judged that he was probably the best-known figure in the group and he was not known at all. Basically, the lineup was listless, so listless in a couple of places it had broken down entirely and the occupants of the positions were lying on the bare tiles, white ankles exposed, either near coma from powerful inhalation or resting in order to improve the quality and strength of their blood. The men themselves insisted their position was in the interests of the latter, but Jack judged the truth to have been nearer the former after an attendant burst through a side door, aroused the sleepers and hustle them from the building.

"Can't have that kind of hanging around here," the man said apologetically to Jack and another newcomer as he returned to whatever position he occupied behind the door. Jack was not especially pleased that he shaped up as socially acceptable to the blood bank crowd, but admitted to himself that it was probably better than rejection.

"You have to watch the needle marks on your arms," the man in front of Jack explained in a kindly, educated manner. "You'd be surprised how many police officers won't believe you're a professional blood donor."

Actually, Jack would not have been surprised at a policeman's questioning since he found it difficult to understand how he had reached such a position himself. He would not have minded had his past been notched with ruined women and discarded fortunes, but to have traveled from nowhere to less than nowhere seemed—to him—a cruel reward. Instead of a lifetime of foul drink and dubious folly, he had been driven to degrading postures in ill-kempt alignments by boredom and nonsensical dreams. He was, Jack realized, not even a romantic wreck.

Contributing his blood was more ordeal than lark. Chagrined at first that he did not possess a rare type, Jack was further startled at the brusqueness of the physical examination, the nausea of the deed, and the banality of the payoff. He was not, however, disheartened by an act that had increased his assets by fifteen dollars, enough cash to attain financial independence and pump color into his pale cheeks and melancholy mood.

Later, Jack shepherded his wardrobe along until almost all of it was laundered, clean and suitable for folding into neat squares and oblongs. He added a jar of peanut butter, some plastic utensils and two packages of raisin cookies to his store of possessions and, finally, on a California-smelling day, with the widow in the backyard improving her flawless suntan, Jack Desbrough departed. He considered leaving a note, a farewell, a ticket to return. But in the end, left nothing but recollections of himself. The gestureless gesture.

17

LEFT TO HIS OWN selection of transportation, Jack certainly would not have imposed himself upon the offers of complete strangers. Hitchhiking contained little or no appeal for him. Placed in any perspective, he considered the endeavor no more pleasurable than a medley of embarrassing rashes or a publicized arrest for a particularly mediocre or unsuccessful crime.

Whenever no formal transportation was available, Jack's inclination had been to decline the opportunity to view mechanical or natural wonders. Nevertheless, he stood near a freeway's entrance, straddling his suitcase, too proud to solicit a ride, relying instead on the native curiosity and intelligence of the American driver to determine what he had in mind. To project an appearance of nonchalance, Jack held a book in one hand as though his interest was literary rather than conveyance. He could not, truthfully, have been less interested in the subject, having spent a period of his life reading and having absorbed all the pursuit had to offer. Although Jack could not plead for a ride employing traditional methods, he had established minimum standards for any that might be tendered. He would reject cattle and chemical trucks, consider small families, and encourage lonely matrons in expensive automobiles. Jack believed that something would always happen, sometimes something good. For that reason, he was only slightly discouraged when he failed to attract a single patron during the early hours of his vigilance.

The first person to actually speak to him was a chubby policeman, constructed in a manner once considered comical but later fashionable among certain individuals engaged in law enforcement, great pouches of power thrust forward. Jack was assuredly nonplussed at being considered a suspicious person, but realized the officer was merely doing his duty and was authorized to act the mean son of a bitch. As a citizen, Jack wondered why the policeman was not more involved in the pursuit of counterfeiters and anarchist malcontents. He questioned the logic of locating illicit operatives on the brink of a major highway, suspecting that even highwaymen did not linger around highways. Jack kept these and other suspicions to himself, even when the policeman returned his meager identification and warned Jack, cheerfully, that he must vacate the city and the area or risk assault by police dogs and city ordinances. Jack accepted the offer to depart without comment and walked away, sullen, passing his heavy suitcase back and forth between his hands.

Circumstances had forced him to amend his standards and Jack was now determined to beat his way eastward, preferably to Philadelphia, as swiftly as possible. During the course of his reading, writing and listening, he had discovered that Philadelphia was probably the city most nearly meeting his needs. Many stories and anthologies dwelt upon the dreariness of existence in that city, and Jack was convinced the atmosphere would be exactly right for the display of his abilities, whatever they were going to be.

Jack resumed his Philadelphia stance, still seemingly distracted, to await his first ride. He had walked a few miles now so his feet were sore from the walking and his hands were sore from carrying the suitcase. Oddly, or perhaps appropriately, the new location proved fortunate for his plans. Jack stood near the storm of automobiles for less than thirty minutes before a young Japanese man driving an aging Jaguar sedan stopped for him. Actually, Jack had to assume the man was Japanese, making the judgment from an Asian appearance and accent as the driver swirled the Jaguar around the cloverleaf, wriggled through angry lines of traffic and emerged free on the freeway.

"I don't like to see anybody in front of me," the Japanese Jaguar driver said. He wore slick, caramel-colored gloves, tight to the bone, and goggles he constantly flipped up or down in a rhythm that puzzled Jack. The driver struggled and fought with the highway even as they broke away from the city's traffic and dashed eastward through the great desert. Whenever the Japanese saw a vehicle ahead he bore down furiously, frequently frightening the driver of the other automobile into skidding off into a dusty escape on the shoulder of the pavement. Others were threatened by a suicidal exhibition of tailgating until the oncoming traffic cleared and the Japanese and Jack could flash past, the Japanese honking the horn with the underside of his wrist.

The Japanese said he was a rodeo cowboy who had been barred from the circuit, "because I don't take nothing from any animals." Now he planned to find work in Las Vegas, probably as an exotic attraction on a Mafia-controlled dude ranch. Jack was surprised to encounter a Japanese cowboy interested in racketeering, but not surprised enough to question the man. He was, actually, prepared to doze off; but the Japanese began reciting a series of anti-Asian anecdotes. The Japanese told these with a sneer on his face and Jack could not determine whether

141

he was expected to laugh good heartedly or express concern at the ethnic implications. He chose to do neither and, eventually, the Japanese suggested the two of them drive to Reno rather than Las Vegas, a suggestions Jack accepted, determining from a map the unexpected diversion would place him squarely on one route to Philadelphia.

The Japanese was an excellent driver, apparently intent on maintaining a pace and schedule carefully charted in his well-ordered mind. Jack realized he had been selected as the observer of his precision. He accepted the role, but declined comment whenever the Japanese passed some landmark and recorded it with a significance glance at his intricate wrist watch, a mechanism constantly humming and buzzing and clicking.

The Japanese drove the hundreds of miles to Reno in an extraordinarily brief time, arriving in the city shortly after sunset. He purchased shoe shines for Jack and himself, then the two of them walked into a busy casino, not quite a parade but a likely pair nonetheless. Recalling the adventures of Joseph and Albert, Jack trusted neither man nor machine in the place. Despite his fascination for tawdry glamour, he was instantly suspicious of an enterprise so well lighted. The entire décor and atmosphere seemed to consist of glare and Jack discovered the women present were preoccupied with money, harboring small cups filled with nickels and dimes and paying brief or no attention to him.

Jack's Japanese benefactor suggested they play manly games, including the smoking of cigars, but when Jack insisted he was departing the Japanese cheerfully drove him through the city and miles beyond before leaving him on the edge of a darkened highway.

Once he was alone in the desert, Jack could think of a great deal of advice he might have accepted. He did not mind being lonely, he even liked the feeling, but he disliked wasting his life loitering near deserted pavement, observed by whatever wind-crazed beasts were creeping about the gloomy premises.

Traffic was sparse and Nevada-like. Only two vehicles passed during the first hour. The desert was also quiet, indicating to Jack that it was crawling with creatures waiting for him to falter or slump over in his tracks, frozen and then devoured in a dry and dusty Yukon, victim of the desert equivalent of giant crabs. Jack did not plan to give the beasts the satisfaction.

This unspoken vow aroused him slightly even though Jack was not the sort to display emotion at the shouts of a crowd, the silence of a mental or physical emptiness, the flinging and falling of stars, or even of his own wisdom. As a matter of fact, he had resigned himself to a dreary night, interrupted by the trampling of tarantulas, when a ratty old Chevrolet sedan rushed past and suddenly, unexpectedly, stopped thirty yards beyond his station.

Jack thought the automobile might have backed up for him easily enough, but he had no real complaint as he ran, slowly, toward his new benefactor, the suitcase handle rolling in his hand and irritating his new calluses and blisters, souvenirs of the chubby cop.

When Jack reached the Chevrolet, he was immediately dismayed at the vehicle's appearance, inside and outside. The sedan had been tackily restored to operating order by the crudest of backyard engineering. A rear side window was missing and had been replace by a plywood panel, albeit one cunningly shaped, the right front fender was an odd tint of green that did not nearly match the cream-colored body, various appurtenances appeared wired on, mostly with odd-sized wiring. The overall effect indicated the hand and toil of the alley scavenger, the coat-hanger craftsman.

The inside of the automobile—both on the floorboard and in the rear seat—was littered with tools and clothing that appeared to have been discarded in untidy haste, perhaps in minor explosion. There were pieces of scrap iron and pipe, some of the metal rusted and unlovable. It appeared the driver might have stolen a windmill.

The driver himself was one of the few items that did match. He seemed precisely the sort of man who would own an automobile like the Chevrolet. His eyes were set back from reddened lids. His clothing and hair were crumpled and unkempt. He appeared ill-fed, or at least, infrequently fed. He was grouchy and touchy.

"Get in," the driver said, grumpily, as Jack probed the rear seat for a place to lodge his suitcase. Even the passenger seat had to be cleared of a collection of debris that—seemingly—had never had any other function than serving as debris.

"I don't usually pick up anybody at night," the driver said, without explaining why he had stopped for Jack, an explanation Jack himself did not require. "I'm going to Tucson," the man continued. The destination did not dismay Jack even as he realized he would be losing several hundred miles on his route to Philadelphia a dubious success in his scheme for success-ful hitch-hiking. Fortunately, the Miracle of Highways is that there are so many of them, all going somewhere.

The driver appeared on the verge of absolute fatigue. He drove with his head leaning on the window, relying on the cold glass and irregularities in the pavement to keep himself awake. Occasionally, he would lower his window and extend his head outside for a refreshing blast of cooled air. Jack volunteered to drive, but the driver said nobody ever touched one of his vehicles, not even the best drivers in the world, naming sev-eral famous names who could not hope to raise enough money to place their hands on the steering wheel. The man seemed extraordinarily proud of his possession, boasting of the bar-gain he had struck with a used car dealer in Portland, Oregon, an unfortunate he indicated had had sedatives

144

and brandy administered to himself when the Chevrolet was removed from his lot. The driver glanced craftily at Jack and insisted Jack estimate the worth of the finely-tuned machine.

Jack guessed the vehicle had cost a thousand dollars and the driver cackled gleefully. "A hundred and twenty dollars," he shouted. "A hundred and twenty dollars is what I paid." The price seemed reasonable enough to Jack, who had never spent a great deal of time in any of the marketplaces and had never owned an automobile.

The driver said his name was Simmons and Jack said his name was Jack. After an hour's driving, Simmons abruptly stopped the Chevrolet in the middle of the highway and motioned Jack outside. Jack assumed he was being evicted from the automobile and possibly slain by knife or gun, so he prepared to collect his suitcase and defend his person with a length of angle iron from the backseat. Simmons lurched from his side of the vehicle and began to throw items around in the trunk, finally emerging with a bottle of Southern Comfort tucked beneath a pile of United States Army blankets.

"That's a woman's drink," Simmons assured Jack as he handed him the bottle, "but a man can drink it too." Jack swallowed a mouthful of the warmth and agreed with Simmons that it was good. After Simmons had secured the bottle in the blankets again—explaining, "No Law's going to catch me with liquor"—the two of them returned, encouraged, to the Chevrolet.

The drink seemed to gentle Simmons and he began to relate episodes from his life, adding items of advice about possible employment on pipe lines and promising instant Hell and Trouble to his former wife should she ever accidentally find him and attempt to collect overdue alimony, child support or forgotten anniversary presents.

Every thirty minutes or so thereafter, Simmons would stop the Chevrolet and he would repeat the search of the blankets and continue drinking. Jack could see that within a thousand miles they would become the greatest of friends, good buddies, chums who might wonder from border to border—any border or border—trading cars, bargaining with cheap but beautiful whores, camping out and fearlessly defying wind and sand. For amusement, they turned into the driveway of one of the red-lighted houses set in the darkness beyond the highway. Simmons honked the horn and asked the attendant, "Is this a rabbit ranch?" The attendant, a nervous man who seemed eager to please, replied that, "It might be arranged. Just park your car over there." The man's obsequious response disappointed Jack and Simmons and they drove away sobered, reflective, briefly better men.

At their next stop, for additional Comfort, the travelers stood once again in the middle of the pavement, still seemingly alone in Nevada. They stared at the expanse of sky, both were silent and contemplative. Jack wondered at his place in the scheme of stars. Simmons was not the sort to admire skies, but could not help himself. These stars embraced the countryside and rendered the surrounding darkness insignificant. Once, during the respite, Simmons started to raise the bottle to his mouth, then abruptly paused to look again, the Comfort suspended an inch from anxious, marveling lips.

When they resumed the drive, Simmons seemed embarrassed. He was determined to muffle his recent awe with a renewed period of surliness. He ceased talking and tuned the radio to a series of obnoxious broadcasts. Far away stations drifted into their hearing and Jack listened to the play-by-play re-creation of a Nebraska high school baseball game with artificial cheering, to the auctioning of thousands of pounds of fat stock, to a disc jockey reciting Indian poetry somewhere in the Dakotas, to an

146

amateur tap-dancing contest in Waterloo, Iowa and to a discouraged junior college debate team whose opponent had failed to appear for a confrontation. Simmons was enraged at the bizarre programming and punched the radio with an angered fist, hoping to beat sense and music into the contrary assortment of wires and tubes. Jack thought fondly of Albert and how he could have easily solved the problem, but kept the thought to himself.

The stops for Southern Comfort dwindled and then ceased, but Simmons developed a craving for coffee, a craving that led the two of them into harshly-lighted cafés frequented by men who looked weatherbeaten and windblown and by women who seemed to appeal to that sort of men. Jack averted his gaze from those women who would catch his eye and, after engaging the cash register in trade, risked certain suitable coins in the slot machines. He did not feel he was impressing the slender audience, but wondered what gasps of admiration would issue if they realized how every expended nickel reduced his fortune by an enormous percentage.

"They cleaned me out the last time I was here," Simmons declared when they returned to the Chevrolet from one of these establishments. He seemed greatly pleased at this flaunting of disaster, this stroll through unforgotten lava, and for a brief time entertained Jack with narratives of his remarkable drives across the United States; incredible non-stop marathons from San Francisco to Houston and from Atlanta to New York State. Simmons assured Jack that he could stay awake at the wheel longer than any other living American. Shortly afterward, Simmons returned to his exhausted posture, the left side of his head lying in the window frame as he drove in alternating burst of frightening speed and ridiculous creeping. Jack gained the impression he was in the midst of a record endurance effort by Simmons. The thought produced a feeling more akin to discomfort than to pleasure.

A couple of hours later, the Aurora of Las Vegas appeared on the Southern Horizon, arousing Simmons and exciting them both with visions of illumination. Guided by the fantastic lighting system, Jack and Simmons sped down the darkened highway, neither wanting the other to speak.

In a remarkably short time they were in the midst of the glow. The beams of the Chevrolet's headlights, so important and significant in the desert, were now only whimsical. Crowds of men in expensive suits shopped in all-night string-tie stores, their feet cold in hand-crafted mesh-toed cowboy boots. Women, wearing fantastic weaves of hair resembling famous African waterfalls, darted in and out of drug stores, changing shifts. Rush-hour traffic merged into after-theatre traffic. Weary adventurers plunged coins—some of them precious souvenirs and priceless lucky pieces—into odd receptacles, gallantly shrugging off the failure of water fountains and the inability of bird baths to pay off jackpots, and then, staggering on to the next project. Las Vegas was electric with light, life and living. Electric with electricity. The once marvelous stars disappeared, wiped out of the sky by a grander glitter. Jack immediately sensed that the entire effect was merely a tinseled monument to greed and regretted that neither the tinsel nor the greed was within his grasp. Both Jack and Simmons were struck with the realization that it could not be for them: Simmons so early "cleaned out" by the scalawags at the frontier outpost, Jack so necessarily reduced to penury before he had had the opportunity to weigh the advantages of either system; the stingy or the spend-thrifty. The unfairness of the gross and crude scene and their inability to participate was especially painful to Simmons. He ceased to even look at the activity and thrust himself into a teeth-grinding observation of local traffic regulations.

Motoring through the city had revived Jack, but Simmons slumped even lower in his seat as they drove southward. Simmons' morose countenance sharpened into edges of anger and his knuckles brightened as he grasped the steering wheel. Within a short time the anger seemed to have seeped out of his body, leaving a shell of dwindling resource, a tubeless human being, unpatchable.

The hour was late when Simmons parked in front of an all-night café in Boulder City. He rubbed his already reddened eyes sleepily as they emerged from the Chevrolet and stumbled wearily against the grain of the cold wind. The café was warm, deserted except for the waitress and an invisible cook rattling utensils in the kitchen. Simmons order the coffee then startled Jack by suggesting he solicit a ride from Boulder City. "I think I'll take the other highway," Simmons explained, lying outrageously and angering young Jack Desbrough, even though Jack readily agreed to the plan. He did not like people who did not like him, realizing they had great weaknesses in their character. He held no sympathy for weakness.

A couple—a bearded man and a finely-cushioned woman—entered the café and interrupted Jack's ire. They sat very near Jack and Simmons on the counter stools and the man proceeded to make a number of gestures, grabbings and gatherings at the woman's person, causing her to thrash about and laugh girlishly. The scene fascinated Jack. The couple's sport now increasing his melancholy and reviving memories of Arlene, of his college sweetheart, of the widow in California, and he yearned to place the struggling stranger on his spare list, perhaps right on the counter top, aware that she would certainly enjoy his style more than that of the bearded boor.

149

This reverie was interrupted by the departure of Simmons. Jack did not trust his fleeing friend to leave his suitcase and walked outside behind him. Simmons, however, was already depositing the suitcase on the street. He did not expend any time on words of regret or departure, but backed from the parking place and drove away. Jack was not surprised when Simmons turned the Chevrolet toward the South and proceeded down the original, intended highway. Although no Tucson-bound son of a bitch could ever discourage him, Jack would have admitted he was not encouraged. Nevada again seemed deserted, miles of unused pavement on any side for him. From a corner of the town a few automobile lights approached but all of them wheeled away and turned into the darkness of the side streets as though intentionally avoiding him.

Jack placed his suitcase on the rim of the highway and sought warmth and comfort from the open portico of an establishment that appeared to offer the tackiest products available in a drug store and bait shop. Two hours remained before daylight and during that time Jack realized he was entirely miserable. He would have forgiven Simmons had that odd fellow suffered a warmth of the heart and returned to fetch him, laden with oatmeal cookies—not even his favorite—and a quart of hot chocolate.

Simmons did not re-appear and the only vehicle to pass Jack during the entire time was a large street sweeper, tidying the curbs. Unlikely transportation though Jack had again revised and lowered his standards.

At dawn the community began to arouse itself and signs of a still-animated civilization appeared. More customers, including the street-sweeper driver, arrived at the café. A sleepy-looking young man began the procedures that would lead to the opening of a nearby service stations, an event Jack judged to be of considerable entertainment value in the community. He pitied the owner of a service station in a city without any automobiles to be serviced, but even as he completed the thought the street, already cleaned, became busier. A milk truck passed, clinking with empty containers, and was followed by a series of automobiles occupied by tourists, some of them wide-eyed children who looked at Jack from behind barricades of toys, clothing, small items of luggage, packages of cookies, and souvenir window stickers. Jack returned the stares of the children, contemptuous of their easy transport.

Three hours after daylight, the city remained cold and Jack remained in the city. He walked behind the store he had frequented for so long and unlatched his suitcase. The tightly-packed valise sprang open like a cheap jack-in-the-box, revealing all of Jack's store of provisions and possessions. The resourceful young man prepared himself a breakfast of peanut butter, which he spread on damaged slices of bread with a plastic knife.

Restored to his usual good humor and health, Jack determined to abandon his sterile position. He repacked the suitcase and walked slowly up the hill and beyond a corner that removed him from the sight of Boulder City. A bare, dustless wind pursed him relentlessly, but even the force of the wind could not diminish his view of the grand valley and the great lake beyond. The panorama was suitable for all walks of life, although Jack realized that some of those walks would not be interested, especially those who continued to pass him at rates of speed whose legality he would question.

Within another couple of hours, the heartening effect of the peanut butter sandwich began to fade and so did Jack. He was sleepy as well as windswept and—as he sat on the upturned edge of his suitcase, almost oblivious to the traffic—he day-dreamed of his old beds, the warm coverings of his childhood, the cooler sheets of his adolescence, the hot tin roof over his head. Some melancholy was involved in this reverie, but Jack was not interested in sympathy so much as he was in a place to lie down. As he considered the prospect of crawling into some protective grasses nearby, his attention was distracted by the appearance of a newcomer, a walker approaching around the hill from the direction Jack had so recently traveled.

The stranger was very tall, very thing black man, wearing two hats and a large back-pack bulging with suspicious pockets. The man was assisted in his walking by a gnarled branch from an unidentifiable tree. This curious walking stick seemed to be capped with a silver knob and tip, but as he drew nearer Jack identified the silver as tin foil, presumably residue from the several sticks of gum occupying the ma's mouth.

Responding to Jack's casual wave, the black stranger strolled across the empty highway. After conspicuously moving the boulder of gum into one jaw with his tongue, he asked Jack, "Want some wine?" Jack replied, truthfully, that he did not. During the next few minutes Jack also rejected the offer of a free harmonica lesson and refused to lend his visitor fifty cents, explaining there was no place to spend the money on the mountainside and that he would need all the capital he possessed. The black man said Jack was selfish for turning down a man who had offered him wine and music.

Jack could not dispute this remark, but rather than admit the truth of it he returned to his suitcase and sat down again, rubbing his eyes to induce artificial alertness. The black man said his name was Billy and declared he was not any sort of animal. He said he would prove he did not have a tail if it were not for the prospect of the law patrolling the area. He explained that his wife would drive out and pick them up in a brand new automobile if he called and asked her, but though only an animal would call up a wife in Tucson and ask her to drive so far. He told Jack he did not have any wine anyhow and then walked away, his knobby stick striking the pavement with a rhythmic clatter, its silver tip flaking off and sparkling in the roadside dust.

Jack watched the thin figure of Billy disappear in the distance, dreading the prospect of some eager liberal passing him and stopping for the black man.

There were, however, no prospects for either of them. The highway wound down the mountainside like an enormous spiral staircase. Jack watched Billy progress slowly and steadily for what looked like many miles before his observation was interrupted by the appearance of another ride.

His rescuers were two young couples, poorly dressed and driving a haggard old panel truck, decorated with a grimacing, visibly fanged bobcat's skull on the dashboard and a large German Shepherd dog amidst the boxes and baggage in the rear. Bricks of drying cheese and opened packages of crackers were scattered on the dashboard around the former bobcat. One of the couples was sleeping in the back with the dog when Jack climbed in the front seat with his suitcase.

The couple sharing the seat with Jack was driving in a co-operative manner, the young man handling the steering wheel and the clutch, the young woman manipulating the awkward gear shift. At first, Jack assumed the graceless truck required two people for proper encouragement but soon understood the pair had turned driving into a sort of party, each movement of the steering and shift of gears bringing an elbow or hand, a hip or knee or some other items of flesh into contact with other flesh. Ordinarily, the cleverness of the game might have revived Jack, but he felt whipped by wind, fatigue, cold and disappointment. Only his spirit remained erect and Jack was too sleepy to employ that.

The driving couple, between giggles, told Jack they were en route to land, willed to the dozing youth by deceased relatives. The four of them would plant watermelons, rose bushes, evergreen trees and anything else that would grow. Unloved earth would become towering forest and flowering glade. Jack considered them optimistic in their forecast of Arizona greenery, but did not speak in discouraging ways. As a matter of fact, he did not have time to respond before the truck pulled up behind Billy, the plodding black man.

The woman, still assisting with the driving, said, "If it was my mother we'd make room," and the young man obligingly braked the truck to a squeaking slide, handling the woman's knee to complete the task. Billy tossed his walking stick aside— the thing no longer silver on either end—and crawled into the truck, displaying no surprise at finding Jack already established.

Billy expressed disgust at the cheese and crackers offered him. "I need some meat," he said biting into a cheese and cracker sandwich. He remained in the truck to eat when they stopped at Hoover Dam to stare at the concrete, and asked for money when they resumed the journey. "Seventy-five cents isn't very much from five people," Billy said, a remark that Jack assumed was directed at him since he had not contributed at all.

The driving couple, Jack, and Billy all crowded uncomfortably on the front seat of the truck, wedged so tightly Jack had to place his arms behind Billy and the young woman, who were on either side of him.

Despite Billy's monologue concerning immense wealth and a loving wife in Tucson, Jack quickly drifted off into sleep and during one of his pleasant dreams his arms slammed down the back of the young woman and the nape of Billy's neck. The accidental blow shocked both victims—Jack could under-stand their feelings—and Billy withdrew into an uneasy quiet, mumbling at fitful intervals and gazing ahead with a cracker in his mouth and moisture in his eyes. When the truck required gasoline and pulled into a shaded service station, Billy reclaimed his knapsack and stalked up the highway without a word of farewell, lonelier than ever now that he was apart from his walking stick.

When they departed the service stations and passed Billy again, he was standing on the opposite side of the highway, either ignoring them as them as thoroughly as possible or planning a return to Nevada. Regardless of his decision, Billy would obviously be altered by a new rancor. Jack felt somewhat disconsolate at his role in the tragedy, but felt even more disconsolate over his lack of sleep. Billy's absence left a great deal more room for relaxation so Jack closed his eyes knowing he yearned for his own alertness for than he deplored Billy's dismay.

Jack slept for only a short time before the truck stopped at a crossroads and he was again on his own. Sleep had been so restful in the truck, Jack decided he would enjoy more. He walked from the highway to a small clump of grass and trees, the tree an unexpected pleasure in this part of the Arizona desert. He ate several of his cookies and then lay down in the shaded grass and weeds. When he awoke, he had forgotten Billy and other unpleasantness. The afternoon was still cool, but the wind and traffic had none of the menace and meanness he had deplored on the Boulder City hillside. The depressed Jack was gone, the fed and comforted Jack had returned, confident he could master the hard pavements as well as the hard cases.

Jack's renewed vigor was not, fortunately, lost on the remainder of the world. He had just resumed his waiting on the highway and barely completed a new arrangement of the contents of his suitcase when a young man in a small automobile stopped in a dusty cloud. The vehicle's radio was turned up so loudly Jack did not have an opportunity to ask where they were going. The direction was suitable and he accepted that reality as reason enough to resume his journey.

Despite the noise, Jack remained drowsy and might have slept again except for a fascination with the driver's technique. The young man was barefoot, manipulating his pedals and arranging his speed with powerful toes. The toes, in turn, were protected by thick, strong nails, more like small turtle's backs. Jack could imagine "Souvenir of Reptile Gardens" painted on them. Consequently, he had no questions when they began stopping at a series of just such establishments.

Jack's new driver did not ignore any attraction, no matter how feeble or mundane. An unfortunate frost had killed all the snakes at Phil's Food 'N Fun, but the proud owner had turned the tables on disaster. He kept the snakes, chilled nearly rigid, in his refrigerated showcase, each one posing as a divider neatly separating the hoop cheeses from the cellophane-wrapped packages of bologna.

Another service station's enormous flashing electric sign advertised cut-rate Indian curios, charred skulls of many animals, and similar oddities. The owner apologized for having sold all his curios then proudly encouraged his young daughter to display her embroidery and play "Under the Double Eagle" on a piano so small Jack assumed it had once been a toy. He wondered why the man did not revise his sign to advertise embroidery displays and piano recitals, but the owner said Jack obviously did not understand the competitiveness of the U.S. Highway 66 business.

"Everybody's got something to show," the young driver said when they resumed their travels. "Some places you got to make them show it, but not on this highway."

Unfortunately, Jack did not share the driver's fascination with the marvels of the avenue and began to dread the sigh of every billboard and coming attraction. Within the next six hours he looked at enough caged armadillos, turquoise jewelry, and second-hand goldmine maps to satisfy a lifetime's curiosity,

156

especially considering he had never been curious about any of them.

Jack would have liked to share his new companion's enthusiasm. "Great," the young man would say following each stop. "That was really great," he usually added. The driver said Route 66 was akin to a two-thousand-mile-long museum, better even than Chicago or the New York's World's Fair of either 1939 or 1940.

If this was true, Jack reflected, he would have to pass up both of those attractions. Certainly neither of them were likely to appear on the outline of the life he had once composed, each year divided into quarters and each quarter containing a list of the accomplishments he intended to complete and the amusements he intended to see. The list was remarkably thorough, an admirable production. Jack only regretted that his life did not resemble his chart. With the slightest flavoring of dismay, he noted that in the place he had penciled in mountaineering he was now inspecting artificial rabbits large enough to mount and pose upon for photographs; during the time he planned the route of a long, lonely journey on a Mexican train he had been rolling down a desert highway listening to a high school softball game.

Disgust, directed at his maudlin sympathy for himself, now wounded his thoughts and Jack struggled to repress the feeling. His new friend, delighted with the crass and trivial, was alive. Jack, possessed by daydreams and ideals, was sinking beyond the sight of the life guards. Even if they attempted to save him, he suspected he might try to fight them off.

"I think I'll get out here," Jack told the young man when they arrived in Albuquerque. The driver was surprised, declaring there were still many great things to see, but Jack had had enough of souvenir tomahawks, rock gardens, and Gila monsters. Albuquerque, because of his earlier adventure at the Peacock Lounge, was not his idea of an ideal location, but Jack's head ached with distractions and exhibitions. Suddenly he was homesick, drawn toward some serene scene on a green plain. He was young yet, but his spirit was aging. He suspected he might need more sleep.

Instead of the green plain, Jack spent two of his dollars to obtain a bed in an old hotel located in a frayed area of the city's business district. The hotel was serene enough. There was no elevator and in the process of walking about the hallways, Jack could hear pleas, sobs, coughs and snores; but he could have heard those in marbled corridors while in the company of the princes of Morocco. People who could not conduct their lives in silence frequently angered or irritated Jack, but he could understand the despair in one of the voices: expectations of pregnancy and fears of abandonment. He could understand, too, the other corridor stirrings: the creak and scrape of someone quietly shifting furniture, the faintly discernable scratching of a writer (suicide notes, menus, poems?), the winding of clocks and the clicking of lamps, the ruffling of pillows. A few of the doors reflected no sound at all and Jack wondered most of all about them. Were they vacant or was some dreadful smothering in progress?

18

THE LOBBY of the hotel in Albuquerque was only slightly larger than the living room of the widow's boarding house in California although it was considerably larger. The darkness was not the pleasant envelope that cloaks all during the hours of the evening, but was a dank, depressing gloom like the tomb of an obscure pharaoh centuries after the last resin-fueled torch has flickered out and its flaking ashes grown cold.

Only by looking toward the plate-glass windows and seeing a framework of bright sunshine blaring around the drawn curtains could Jack even be certain daylight was in progress. The curtains, dusty as they were, brought a breadth of familiarity to Jack's senses. They looked and smelled like the United States Army blankets Simmons had folded in the trunk of his automobile to cradle and conceal his bottle of Southern Comfort. The recollection did not make Jack yearn for another version of Simmons to appear—he had all but forgotten the mountainside at Boulder City—but did remind him he should be moving on to Cleveland or Pittsburgh or some other city with prominent baseball and noisy streetcars rattling down the avenues. He was not especially attracted by either, but assumed they marked boundaries he should establish for himself.

For the moment, Jack wondered why he would be concerned about the time of day. He was, he estimated, an experienced traveler, one who knew things would never remain the same no matter the hours he lingered or the locations he visited. He supposed there was an algebraic equation he might apply to calculate exactly how long he would occupy one position before events swept him into the tide that always ebbs except when it flows. He determined—without this calculation—that he would not wait for the flow.

Except for the desk clerk, asleep with his nearly-bald head lying on the equally-bared registration desk, only one other person was in the lobby. He was a roosterish little man sitting on a tufted chair beneath a dimly-glowing lamp. He was holding a newspaper folded into a narrow rectangle in the fashion of a racetrack tout stranded thousands of miles from his track. Jack approached the little man's chair in the way of a mendicant seeking instruction on future races or future lives. In a manner of speaking, that was exactly what he was although the advice Jack sought was concerned with procedures for hitchhiking away from downtown Albuquerque. Already, the handles on his suitcase had resumed irritating his fingers, leaving Jack with no interest in another police-insisted stroll to the city limit sign.

The roosterish little man, despite his somewhat comical appearance, was neither good-humored nor helpful. Jack expected witty epigrams and big city wisecracks, maybe even some Bicycle Bob-type advice in response to his inquiries; not the grumpy reply that ensued. The little man, true to the character suggested by his appearance and Bicycle Bob's warning about roosterish little men, chewed the stub of a long extinguished cigar resembling, it may be repeated, the lifeless torch of a pharaoh's tomb. The end of the cigar in his mouth was moist to the appearance of brown mush. The little man bit into this stub as he studied Jack over the edge of his newspaper. Jack noticed that the paper was folded into the comic strips. With only a bit more light from the lamp, he might well have read *Barney Google* or *Snuffy Smith* to himself.

"Do I look like a goddamned information booth?" the little man growled rudely. "Go see Travelers' Aid. They like giving information to bums."

Jack recalled that he once did not consider himself a hobo and now did not consider himself a tramp or a bum, but refrained from a natural impulse to punch the roosterish little man, reasoning he could ill afford additional damage to already sore hands.

The Traveler's Aid was located in the same seedy neighborhood as the hotel, its front door sheltered from the intense sun by the marquee of a decaying downtown movie theater, another of the seemingly endless reminders of Jack's California days—days he was growing to regret, though they seemed as distant as Goldsmith or the playground swing occupied by Arlene.

The theater's box office was closed. Its three windows were shuttered. But posters advertised *Boston Blackie* and *Hopalong Cassidy* features, two favorites of Jack. There was a time when he could not determine which of his ambitions was greater. To accommodate his daydreams he devised a game involving both his heroes as well as constant gun play; those innocent days when he could blow the brains out of anyone who crossed his path: friend, foe, or fantasy.

The wall between the movie theater and the Travel Bureau was thin, only slightly thicker and more substantial than cardboard. Jack could see a large, circular grease stain where he assumed the concession stand and its popcorn machine was located on the theater side of the wall. The concentrated smell of aged popcorn pervaded the premises and supported this thought. A few men

161

lounged on crude wooden benches placed against one wall and other men sat on folded chairs in the middle of the room. Some of the men dozed off, others mumbled together in presumed conversation. Two of them stood shoulder-to-shoulder at the long desk running the width of the bureau, dividing the ins from the outs. These men seemed to be poring over a map spread on the counter while the agent looked at them, balefully, from beneath a greenish eyeshade. The agent also had leather bands around his bicep and leather cuffs on both wrists as though engaged in a more desperate endeavor than encouraging vagrants to vacate the city.

Jack sat by himself on one of the benches, facing the grease spot, and began reading bedraggled, outdated copies of *Police Gazette* and *Billboard*. From this material he deduced the bureau appealed mostly to criminals who favored 1930's chorus girls and idle carnival workers seeking employment on winter circuits. The men he saw fell into either of these categories, but they would also fit into the blood bank crowd he encountered in Los Angeles. Jack could see the same bare, bony ankles. He attempted to view some of the forearms, but most of the men wore coats and all of them were in long sleeves. Instead, he inspected his own forearms as though expecting to identify insinuating marks.

The two men at the counter departed out the door so Jack arose from his position on the bench and approached the newly idled, still eye-shaded authority.

"I need to leave Albuquerque," Jack told the agent. The man looked from beneath his shade but displayed no other acknowledgement beyond a slightly raised eyebrow. "I heard you could help," Jack added, recognizing the lameness in his own voice.

"Can't help nobody fleeing a felony," the agent finally responded, as though dismissing any conception of aid or assistance.

"I'm not fleeing anything…"

"Sure you are, son. Everybody's fleeing something, else they wouldn't be wanting to leave. One goddamn, godforsaken dump is just like any other one. Change the name of the trees is the only way you can tell Mesquite, Texas from Oak Park, Illinois."

"Is this the help you give everybody? This doesn't seem like travelers aid to me."

"Don't take it personal, son. Tell that to everybody. Be certain they really want to go. Besides, how do you know what aid is? I might have just give you the best advice you'll ever get. That's up to you. Where you want to go? We got cars and drivers travelin' in ever direction there is. More directions than you ever heard about. If it's not today, it'll be tomorrow. Hell, we got a regular run to Fairbanks, Alaska carryin' a load of serum to the poor, lamed orphans. Lot of people want to make that trip. Enjoy the Alcan Highway. Pothole free maybe. Not bear free. See the goats in the Rockies, watch Eskimo gals rassle in a barrel of blubber, help the little orphan fellers. Help the hell out of them. Most of them don't even know they want the serum. It teaches you a lot about the facts of life."

Jack assumed the man was being whimsical. He had long ago abandoned any thoughts of travel to Alaska and no longer possessed an address for Joseph and Albert, realizing such an address was unlikely to be valid for more than a week. For all he knew, they were even now in Albuquerque at Pearl's Place or the Peacock Lounge.

"I wouldn't mind Philadelphia," Jack said.

"Philadelphia, P.A... Haven't had a Philadelphia, P.A. in a long time. Not a problem though. Lot of cars going to Manhattan, New York. Drop you off on the way. Right on Chestnut Street. Been there myself. Didn't like it. Don't like anywhere except Albuquerque. The only town with two Q's and two U's in its name. Unless you count Quitaque and nobody outside of Texas knows where that is. Hell, some of them inside

163

Texas don't know where it is. Don't even like the rest of New Mexico or some parts of Albuquerque for that matter. I'll see what we can do for you. You never know. Best ride out of here I know of was about five years ago. Rich, fat old gal wanted somebody to drive her all the way to Providence, Rhode Island. She had some bucks, but she was a mess. Big old flabby stomach. Fat rolled off of her like an avalanche of lard. Smelled like she made all of her money by being inside woman on a hog farm. Said she'd pay all expenses and she'd give the Cadillac to anybody who showed her some lovin' and a good time. No sir, not many come along like that."

"I guess not. I'm not expecting anything like that."

"Neither was I. That's why I took it myself. Even after I got in the car and looked at that old gal. She was sweatin' like she was tryin' out for the Mizziz B.O. contest and that was her talent. There was even drops of sweat on that little mustache she had and on the hair that poked out of the mole on her nose. You know I hadn't had that Cadillac hardly but two weeks when I totaled it out on the highway to Taos. I always say it's bad luck to be lucky."

Jack began to think the agent was some sort of ass dedicated to foiling any attempts to motor out of Albuquerque, more like an anti-travel agent. He wondered if other clients had encountered a similar reception and glanced, surreptitiously, about the premises to see if any of the other men were aware of his situation. None were paying any attention. There were still the dozers, one now with bath agape. Two other men stared vacantly into space, like twins foreseeing their own routes to far distant fates or futures. Still another man in a straw hat had set up a chess game from a small set he apparently could carry in his pocket, the miniature knights and pawns poised perfectly on the board he had placed on a vacant folding chair he had converted into a game table. No one edged forward to occupy the place obviously reserved for an opponent so the chess hopeful became the first to actually catch Jack's eye. Quickly, Jack looked away. He preferred the cackling manipulations of the agent to any hopeful pleading for a hint of comradeship or even an hour or so of subtle competition. Jack thought of the lonesome kid in the schoolyard at Goldsmith so many million miles and memories in the past. "I'm not that kid," he told himself.

"It doesn't have to be Philadelphia," he told the agent. "I'll go just about anywhere."

"Got cars bound for Little Rock and Big Spring this afternoon. One you have to baby sit twin boys three years old. Know anything about diapers? Know anything about crying? The other you got to drive all night and share gas expenses. Got any money? Ever get sleepy? Better not have too much money. We guarantee some transportation. We don't guarantee safe arrival."

"That's not a problem. I've never had too much money."

"A good thing. Best way to avoid temptation. Yours and the other fellows. Check back in a few hours. We got cars going in every direction. Got a regular run to Fairbanks, Alaska."

"You already told me about that."

"Did I tell you about the old gal going to Baltimore?"

"The same one going to Providence, Rhode Island?"

"Nah. That was her sister...But it's the same story."

"Yes, you told me."

"The good thing about my stories is folks want to hear them more than once."

* * *

Neither Joseph nor Albert had subscribed to many of society's conventions, certainly not to the one demanding payment of admission fees for any sort of amusement whether games or concerts or world's fairs. The pair had devised methods for

165

gaining entry to nearly any sort of entertainment arena and shared some of them during their brief sojourn with Jack. He preferred the simple, cleanly efficient ones like joining a crowd rushing and jostling a harried gate keeper and acting as though they had proffered tickets. He did not like the complex, sometimes disgusting ones like crawling through filthy heating and air conditioning ducts, and he hated the pleading and begging scenes. The one he had mastered and employed now involved taking advantage of the emergency exits of small movie theaters. They were always at the rear of the building, usually in a sheltered alley. Springing the door open was simple enough, those functioning correctly were engineered to open easily, although daytime entry produced a bolt of sunlight alerting the entire attendance to an intrusion. As Albert explained this was a negligible consequence. Even theaters with names like Grand and Palace rarely employed ushers during the weekday matinee performances and the audience was so rapt in its interpretations of filmed dreams, the odds of betrayal were small and the penalties minor. On one occasion, Joseph had been evicted from a Burbank theater objecting and protesting so loudly the management actually refunded the admission charges. Jack realized he could never engage in that noisy tactic but now he considered asking for a refund when the second feature was a Bulldog Drummond instead of a Boston Blackie. He disliked being cheated or misled. Even worse would have been a double feature of all foreign films Charlie Chan and the Cisco Kid.

* * *

The Travel Bureau agent seemed pleased, even eager, to see Jack when he returned. "Sometimes I feel like a damned magician performing tricks instead of the Good Samaritan that I usually am," he said. "I got you an automobile leaving

166

for Princeton, New Jersey, tomorrow morning at six o'clock in the a.m. Going right through Philadelphia. Plans to stop there to visit an old auntie. He's about your age. Wants help driving and staying awake. I told him you was a first-class driver and had a friendly personality. Maybe you can fake one of them."

"I can drive okay."

"You'll be in a nineteen-fifty Mercury coupe. He's got an air-conditioner rigged up in one window so half your face will be cold all the way to Pennsylvania. You'll think you're in Fairbanks. By this time tomorrow evening you'll be out of the desert. You won't be able to see the scenery for all the hills and trees. John Law 'll be miles behind you."

"John Law's not looking for me."

"That's the way, son. Don't change your story for nobody. Even if he's the miracle worker got you a ride."

* * *

Jack's new friend was prompt, arriving in front of the Travel Bureau at almost precisely six a.m. No other persons were visible on the street. This part of Albuquerque was almost as quiet and deserted as Boulder City at the same hour. So familiar was the scene Jack half expected to see a street sweeper busily at work or hear a dairy truck rattling bottles around a corner, but his only companion during his half hour wait was a gray-and-black striped cat which clambered out of a storm drain to inspect the garbage swept out of the movie theater and into the gutter. The pickings were slim, only stray bits of popcorn and nearly-melted chocolate, but they seemed to be what the cat was scratching for. He brushed himself casually against the back of Jack's right leg but dismissed a possible pat and disappeared back into is underground chamber. Jack speculated on this life, only to reflect that it was not so far removed from his own.

167

Jack was pleased by the sight of the Mercury as it eased to the curb where he stood. Although the vehicle was not a new Cadillac driven by an overweight coquette it was a nearly-new automobile, silvery gray in color, almost like the recent cat, driven by a young man, handsome in the manner of Steve Hatfield. The young man sprang from the Mercury to unlock the trunk, pausing to shake Jack's hand enthusiastically before hefting Jack's suitcase into an empty space, seemingly into an area specifically appointed for the purpose. Jack regarded the young man's button-down blue collar shirt; his neatly combed, short haircut; the precise mold of his khaki trousers and determined the placement of the suitcase was not so much good fortune as the result of a mind of such precise order the young man did not have to formulate plans in advance. Nothing in the next two day's conversation caused Jack to revise this initial impression.

The young man's name was John Quincy Booth, the result, he said, of being a member of a family claiming to be related to both a president and a presidential assassin. Jack was to call him John, as his family did, or J.Q. as most of his Princeton classmates did. "J.Q. rhymes with Jehu. He was a biblical general and king and a hell of a charioteer. Like the school song. He's not that famous unless you read the Old Testament Kings. I like that part too." Jack personally had no preference. "John or J.Q. makes no difference. Names are for tombstones. The marker I'm going to have won't be anywhere it can be read by people."

Jack was puzzled by the latter remark, but J.Q. seemed unperturbed by the projected future. Jack did not require an explanation although he arrived at his own conclusions as the miles began to recede in the West.

On the first day they drove from Albuquerque to Oklahoma City, changing drivers first at Moriarty and then at Amarillo.

J.Q. questioned the presumption of a state having a town named Moriarty but not one named Holmes. Jack said he supposed it was another of life's unsolvable mysteries. "Ha," said J.Q.

During his turns at the steering wheel J.Q. pushed the accelerator to racetrack speeds, faster even than the Japanese cowboy although he did not approach other automobiles with the same kamikaze frenzy. He even slowed imperceptibly when passing other vehicles on a curve, a concession to reduced impact Jack felt only mildly comforting. Jack did not protest, but did ask if they were in some sort of a rush.

"Only like every day," J.Q. replied. "We're all sentenced to death row and there's not going to be any appeal or any reprieves. There'll be a last meal and a last word. You can't be waiting around or slowing up." Jack was not charting, but if he had been he would have list this as among J.Q.'s cheerful pessimisms. He seemed to have a Princeton man's steamer trunk full of them, the overflow pasted like travel decals on the trunk's shell.

J.Q. would be graduating in another year then planned to enroll in a program at the University of Pennsylvania which would result in both law and medical degrees. "The only hard thing about medical school is memorizing the anatomy. The only thing difficult about law school is remembering that two wrongs frequently make a right. They'll be easy for me. I can remember things."

Jack said he had never known a doctor who was also a lawyer.

"There won't be one when I'm finished either," J.Q. said. "You'd think I was going to heal the cheated and sue the sick, but I'm not. I'm going to South America and disappear in the Amazon jungle. It'll be my personal Diaspora. You won't hear my name again until I'm successful. The Booths have always believed in the plantation system. It works best for everybody. Heck, it built Newport and it financed a war, two things anybody can believe in. I'm going to have a plantation of my own. They'll be talking about me the way they talk about Jay Gould or the Rockefellers. I'm going to be a Rubber Baron."

Jack's impression of the Amazon and its tributaries was limited enormous snakes lurking in the trees and murky waters thickened even murkier by enormous fish, but despite these images he was impressed by J.Q.'s plans for himself. No one, not Joseph or Albert, Max Murphy, or Steve Hatfield and certainly not himself had plotted out a future so thoroughly, as though life could be arranged with a T-square and a slide rule. He had no doubt J.Q. would do exactly what he said he would do, success beckoning like the lights of Las Vegas even as they sped through Henrietta and Sallisaw.

In some respects, Jack was jealous of John Quincy Booth. He had no interest in establishing a rubber plantation or even in seeing the Amazon River. He had once waded across the Pecos and the prospect of stepping into quicksand was all the discouragement he needed to avoid bodies or streams of water. Swallowed by the earth was a fate for J.Q. Booth, not for himself. He also had no interest in the medical or any other profession either. He did, however, have an interest in himself. Perhaps his future was like quicksand, something to be avoided, but this philosophical dissonance produced no serenity and certainly no ambition. Songs had been written about coal miners and cowboys and locomotive engineers so he contemplated that as he contemplated the fact that there were no songs about doctors or lawyers or bankers or even about rubber plantation owners; noting to himself that the road to obscurity was apparently paved with money and the road to recognition with hard knocks. Neither were appealing goals.

Jack attempted to put these thoughts into conversation with J.Q., but his sentences thinned to the trivial and then to silence. He realized that not only did he not have a future, he could not even express his belief (or dismay) in the futility of having a future.

By the hour they passed from Oklahoma into Arkansas, even J.Q. had been reduced to a similar quietness. Each young man seemed to have exhausted the other. Long gray skies finally opened up just outside of Fort Smith and rain seemed to follow them for every one of the miles across the state. Some of the rain was little more than a drizzle, but much of it was storm driven, water washing over the Mercury in waves the wipers could not begin to subdue. "Lord, we might as well be driving on a river bed," J.Q. said, forecasting—as usual—the contents of the future.

The rain actually slackened its pouring near Stuttgart, but miles of highway remained under water and they seemed to be motoring on a river bed. Men, many in wading boots and other duck hunting gear but mostly in their working overalls stood at intervals along the road, human markers delineating the edge of the highway, waving vehicles forward to the next sentinel. Beyond them, presumably, was a swampish depth that would provide a preview to the Amazon. Cypress trees loomed in the mists of the bleak day. Barkless and knobby-kneed roots were matching or mocking the bare legs and knees of some of the men marking the route. None of these men smiled or waved as Jack and J.Q. and the other slow-moving vehicles sloshed eastward. Swells of water lapped at the waists of the men, but no automobile was moving fast enough to drench them. Jack supposed that was the sort of work that awaited him: A guardian agent against storms, busy on only a few days of the year, but on those days more important, more life-enlarging than any lawyer or physician. Hell, he already had the white shanks.

Gradually, the water on the highway became shallower until they finally emerged onto visible pavement, freed from any claims by whatever river or creek had overflowed. Jack knew he should feel relieved, at least from the boredom of the constant stream.

171

J.Q. recalled that when he was young his parents had taken him and his sister on a transcontinental automobile trip, mostly on the Bankhead Highway but with assorted wanderings to places his father thought might be interesting, traveling from South Carolina to Southern California. "The S.C. route," his father called it.

At Memphis they had crossed the Mississippi River on piggyback wooden planks suspended from the sides of the railroad's Harahan Bridge. The rattletrap contraption swayed and shook as though tearing away from its rivets, the wobbly planks rattling and shaking behind them. "And this skinny little railing was the only thing between us and a hundred foot drop in the river. My sister cried, but I was big boy. I just shut my eyes. My granddad was on the trip. He was nearly ninety years old and he'd been at Chickamauga. He said he'd rather charge barefoot up Missionary Ridge through a field of stinging nettles than drive over that bridge again. My dad said he agreed and we came back home the long way, through Saint Louis. Now, it's sissy time and you can hardly tell when you get off the highway and get on the bridge. Memphis has gone soft. The whole South is going soft. That's why I'm heading for as far south as you can go, to the ends of the earth, to Patagonia or the Amazon. Heck, you can't even cross that river. Today's trip would be more like a nursery rhyme than an adventure story."

Jack had no comment on J.Q.'s remarks, but recalled that the Bankhead Highway wound through Odessa and he might have been standing on a street corner selling newspapers when J.Q. and the other members of the Booth family passed through.

"I remember you," J.Q. said. "I remember my granddad saying, 'Toss a nickel to that cotton-topped ragamuffin'."

"That would have been me," Jack confirmed. "I still have the gum I bought with that nickel."

"You were a wise child and now you're a wise guy."

The two of them signed into the Gayoso Hotel then wandered north on Main Street before strolling back among the cotton warehouses on Front Street. During the walk, Jack noted motion picture theaters as well as streetcars and streetcar tracks. Back at the hotel, he asked the desk clerk if there was baseball in the city. The clerk appeared surprised by the question, apparently fearing he was being set up to appear foolish. "The Memphis Chicks," he replied warily, "Like they've always been."

"If I had a team here, I'd call it the Memphis Blues," Jack said.

"If I had a dime for every time I heard that, I'd own the team," the clerk said. "You can take a streetcar or even walk from here to Russwood Park tomorrow afternoon. If you run into the river, you've gone the wrong way. They'll be playing the Atlanta Crackers."

Jack believed he might have come far enough.

19

OUTSIDE, and in the unwarmed parts of the inside, Jack was cold. The cold was not Joseph and Albert's distant Alaska. It was Southern cold. The winter, bitter as it was, had not shriveled the landscape and turned life motionless even though the night was chilled enough to twist moving figures into the postures of marionettes manipulated by untrained fingers. The time was near a New Year. All that remained of the present were the few hours before midnight. Soon even those hours would pass and events would be different for him, a difference as perceptible as a degree in temperature, evident to none except those who constantly consult thermometers. Jack, himself, rarely did.

Even in a city like Memphis, not really a city, his New Year's celebrations were very like the Fourth of July celebrations, those in turn nearly identical to Birthdays or the weekends without specific titles. Consequently, weather was most important for the future of anecdote and reminiscence. The weather separates the holidays from the Thursdays, the warmth or unwarmth a reminder of the events of days and years past. Years gone by. Years to come.

On a few of these occasions, Jack recognized a definite-ness that sorted them out from the others. A spectacular depravity, an ill-deserved beating, or an applauded success beatified or otherwise impressed the Fifth Day of August in the household of his memory. For other episodes the definiteness was more indefinite, a something or somehow that looped about strangers, drew them together for a time, would not yield to violent spasm, yet released at the slightest hint of emotion.

Two others accompanied Jack at the beginning of this night. All three of them were in the middle years of young manhood, still attempting to recover one adventure from every evening: the legendary pace of life whether from a place at the Round Table or standing at the mouth of the Batcave, or any one of the thousand and one Arabian Nights.

One of the two men had become an almost constant companion of Jack Desbrough. George Songman, as a matter of fact, would be the last of Jack's good friends. They were entirely dissimilar in appearance, but were remarkably similar in other respects. Each was without advertised emotion, tongues coating slowly with their own silences. Often they sat for hours—separated by a few inches of table—without comment except for minimal consultation with a waitress. Over the years, since Jack's arrival in the city, each had learned the other's inclination in wenching, drinking, sentiment.

Sometimes they did speak and on one of these occasions George told Jack he wondered if the day would not come when they would have forgotten how to converse... at least with one another. Jack did not respond to the observation, but in thought's dialogue reminded himself that, with the possible exception of himself, George was the wisest, kindest man he would know.

Accompanying the two friends was a plump acquaintance best known for his resemblance to a famous singer. The acquaintance's style—like the singer's—was an extremely vocal one, his repertoire a once-amusing anthology of stories concerning his

176

high school exploits and bloviated reviews of his own romantic capers, the latter negligible until the singer became popular and made crude gestures and rubeish manners acceptable.

The meeting place was located in an area of the city that would be described as modest in the optimistic prose of real estate literature, containing all the squalor and debris and none of the charm and excitement of a sleazy border town. Within the same block were a wheel aligner, a barber advertising flat-top haircuts as a specialty, a chain liquor store lending agency with early American furniture in the windows, and a drug store of the nondescript drug-store variety.

The tavern itself was employed mostly for dependability and was otherwise without distinguishing marks or scars. The establishment was named Laura's in two places on two windows, but if there had ever been a Laura she could not be recalled by the present management. The lighting was bright, an unfortunate circumstance. The furnishings were plain and the service also plain and poor. The waitresses pleaded for tips. Sometimes demanded them. The décor, frequently altered, depended upon the bent of the brewer's imaginative craftsmen. There were bubbling jets of color, hobbling models of comic automobiles, and gilded globes of another drinking era. Jack's old friends, Joseph and Albert, would never have attended such a place. X.L.Wisenhunt would not have dignified it with either flames or explosives.

All this was of slight knowledge, even slighter interest, to the three as they seated themselves at intervals around a padded corner booth. A minor contest, unnoticed at even the nearest table, determined the better viewing points: facing the door and the room's activity. Those places fell to Jack Desbrough and George Songman.

The three planned to drink the New Year into their lives. From other nights in the same position they knew this could be accomplished. There was no cynicism about them, except for George Songman's seldom spoken fear of the future. "Our future is to have no past," he would say, amused or solemn as the evening demanded. They knew enough beer in an unlimited flow would permit a certain pleasantness to assume prominence and to remain there until the flow ceased at closing time.

Ernest, the man who looked like the famous singer, began the night's voices with his practiced narrative. For all he knew, Jack and George were listening, although both had heard his monologue many times before. He had spent, Ernest declared, three years in a public high school detention hall for throwing a cherry bomb, mixed in corn meal and molasses, onto a teacher's front porch. Three years without lunch or human companionship from 11:30 a.m. until 12:15 p.m.

He had, Ernest continued, mounted a mirror in the inside of a shoe tongue and with the slightest tap of a toe gained a vision of that infrequent wonder beneath a girl's skirt. Scars along the top of his right foot proved the truth of this story and its unhappy conclusion in a crowded hallway.

At 10:33, the three were three beers into the celebration and were joined by a pair of newcomers. One of them, Jerry Salmon, was muscular but extremely small. His size, or the absence of size, was emphasized by his companion, a large man with wide shoulders and a robust chest. His name was J.V. Jacobs and he was suspect among the original three. Jacobs was clean-cut, trim, charming to females, quiet spoken, neatly and fashionably dressed, shoe shined, still another replica of Steve Hatfield. His appearance was the enamel-covered magazine's illusion of the heroic college fullback and he was, in fact, a former college fullback, albeit a mediocre one. Despite his athletic, rough-hewn impression, J.V. Jacobs was crafty, a plotter. Not mediocre at all in the thing he did best. While his mouth spoke pleasantly, Jacob's eyes wandered constantly among the other things—strange, savage beacons at best—which contributed a feeling that his announcements were pre-recorded, and he had no relation to the present tense. George Songman and J.V. Jacobs had been close friends once, until the plots began to develop, without pre-meditation but surely and confidently. Twice, George became involved in them and so gradually edged away from the friendship and toward his silent companion, Jack Desbrough.

Through his fourth beer, J.V. Jacobs related football feats, assuming the conversational leadership from Ernest, who did not actually stop talking but was reduced to a voice of punctuation. Aside from his touchdowns, Jacobs had accumulated fame in a number of locally-remarked bedrooms and automobile cushions, both the front and the back, proving that such success did not require a resemblance to popular entertainers. He maneuvered between the topics in the sly and elusive and cocksure manner of all broken-field runners.

Jack, his dislike for Jacobs driving him to conviviality, became almost gregarious, the rarest of all characters for him. He coaxed Jacobs into a new line of previously-unrelated triumphs, rubbing his teeth with the back of a thumb knuckle, sometimes replacing the thumb with his beer glass, but always keeping one or the other before his face, a matador's tools wielded in the false gloaming.

An obscenity, necessary in masculine reminiscence, reminded Ernest that he once slipped into a classroom, erased a laboriously-chalked final examination from the blackboard and substituted the same word in plain, block letters two feet high.

"When the teacher rolled up the maps and saw it he turned around with tears in his eyes and said if anybody would confess he'd pass them with an 'A' and no questions asked. There was an idiot in there had never passed anything in his life. He held up his hand and sure enough the teacher passed him."

179

Jack steered Jacobs back onto the subject, laughing or not laughing as his thumb shuttled along its ivory course.

While Jack was flattering Jacobs for his own amusement, Jacobs himself began his first project, devoting his eyes to Salmon, known to attempt strange feats when his senses were diluted. Jacobs removed a khaki-colored paper sack from the pocket of his black raincoat and slid most of a green-labeled fifth of Jack Daniels from the sack. He poured a glass half full of the whiskey then pushed the glass toward Salmon who, obviously, had had others.

George Songman, sarcastic, asked, "Why don't you just go ahead and fill it up so you won't have to waste any 7-Up?"

Jacobs leaned across the table, glared at George Songman through the silence, retrieved the glass, poured it near brim level with Jack Daniels, returned the glass to Salmon, then looked back at George, still in the silence.

Disgusted, George Songman twisted over spread legs and walked from the booth to the restroom at the rear of the lounge. J.V. Jacobs stared intently at the gray door, his eyes tracing the lettering in 'Gentlemen.' He told the others, "I like George, but he's the way he is. It's part of his make-up. He's said some things in here tonight I sure don't like. I didn't want to come in here in the first place. I'm about ready to turn around and leave."

Jack did not respond to J.V. Jacob's assertion of wounded feelings, but Jacobs made no move to depart when George returned. The two glared at one another again and Ernest, reminded of trouble, said, "I was sittin' over at Terry's Club in West Memphis when this guy I never saw before comes by and says, 'Don't move my chair again.' I didn't know what he was talking about, but I got his chair and put it on top of a table and sat down. He came back and gave me a rabbit punch and I got up and fought. Goddamn he whipped the hell out of me but it was funny."

180

Two more newcomers joined the table. One, a woman named Martha, was known to them all except J.V. Jacobs. The other was her escort, an effeminate stranger introduced as Brownie from Tulsa, Oklahoma. Laura's was the second attraction on their own tour of the holiday.

Martha asked J.V. Jacobs why he was not drinking.

"Ma'am, I don't drink," Jacobs replied.

"You look like a football player," Brownie said.

"Thank you, sir. That's a compliment. I'm trying to play football at Delta State."

"That's wonderful," Martha said and then asked George Songman how tall he was and how much he weighed. George told her and she said, "I think that's wonderful."

Salmon stood in a grotesque version of attention.

"I'm five feet five and proud of it," he declared defiantly.

Salmon was poised for display. Jacobs told him to jiggle.

The little man required no additional urging and began a slow quiver below the knees. The movement spread at increasing speeds upward through his body until at last, his entire frame was quaking like a model volcano near eruption. The new arrivals watched transfixed, mystified.

When Salmon completed his famous talent, Jacobs stood and departed for the restroom himself. George turned to Jack and said, quietly, "That's the biggest jerk in the world. I could hear what he was telling you a while ago. You saw him pour that drink for Salmon. He's doing it on purpose. He thinks it's funny. Now he'll make Salmon drive home."

Jacobs returned, glared at George, then sat down and directed his attention toward Martha and her companion.

Brownie's presence brought new affluence to the table. He insisted on buying everything. He added popcorn to the rations and paid from a thick fold of currency peeled from a silver money clip molded in the shape of a dollar sign.

Martha, unmarried, had reached a period of sensitivity about her situation. She dwelt on the domestic career as a career and recounted a story of broken hearts which she called broken hearts.

Jacobs, probing for an injection of his famous charm, replied with the mottoes and assurances that had carried him over a hundred skittish flanks in night's past. Martha actually grew cheerful in contemplation of her melancholy.

Brownie registered a complaint of his own. He had recently divorced a wife and was the victim of an unjust decree and an unfaithful woman.

"I fought it because of my son," he said, "but a woman's word is worth five men in court. I have to pay four hundred dollars a month alimony."

Ernest asked Brownie if he had any oil wells.

"Only three."

Midnight arrived and even though twelve o'clock had been the purpose of the evening the group had forgotten the celebration until the club manager blew weakly through a toy horn and shouted, "Happy New Year."

They all looked doubtful, then Ernest also shouted, "Happy New Year," and Martha began kissing each one of them. The kiss had more than enough warmth to be arousing, though not enough to institute assault. When she finished, Martha told Brownie it was time to leave. While Brownie assisted her with her coat, J.V. Jacobs whispered in Martha's ear. She glowed at him and told the others, "This has been the happiest New Year I've spent in years and you charming gentlemen are the reason."

"The pleasure was all ours," Jacobs replied.

When they were gone, Jacobs and Songman resumed the duel of sneers and barbs, weapons expertly employed this late in the drinking and practicing.

182

Finally, reminded of his old schemes, Jacobs asked, "Have I ever fouled you up?"

"Yes," George answered. "How about the times you've got Salmon drunk and left him for me to take care of?"

Since Salmon was already reduced to an irregular giggling, the challenge to his reputation was too obvious for Jacobs to ignore. He shrugged his shoulders, straightening invisible pads, placed a hand firmly under Salmon's elbow and bowed sarcastically.

"This has been the happiest New Year I've spent in years and you charming gentlemen are the reason," he said.

Jacobs and salmon departed, Jacobs balancing the wobbly Salmon and steering him around the tables and out the door. They had barely disappeared into the cold night and the unknown year when Brownie returned. He walked hastily to the table, rubbing his hands to displace the chill. He sat back down among them, looked around and asked, "Where's Jacobs?"

"Don't worry about him," George said. "He's a fruit."

"I just don't understand people sometimes," Brownie said, disappointed. He produced his silver money clip and ordered a replenishment of the beer. Lipstick lingered on the corner of his mouth and the unexpected disorder in his otherwise immaculate appearance disturbed Jack and George. George nudged Jack from the booth toward the chromed juke box, a magnificent machine of buttons and combinations and revolutions per minute.

The machine splashed a blue shadow on their faces as they studied the titles and code numbers. Mose Allison's *Parchman Farm* cast its own shadow over their voices and Jack asked, "What do you think?"

"Let's roll him. I know Ernest will go along. You with us or you chicken?"

Jack studied George's young face to be certain his friend was serious. George was laughing, but not really. He was serious. The idea began to seem a good one.

"I'll be right behind you," Jack said.

"I'll guarantee your cut."

"Be sure you do. I'm not used to this racketeering."

"Bull. You're another Capone. You were born for it."

The two great friends laughed again. This time they were both serious. George Songman punched enough buttons to discharge his quarters and they walked back to the New Year's still-festive table, wet and slippery with spilled beer and gritty with potato chip drippings.

Brownie said he wished Jacobs would return.

Jack looked at Ernest and began to talk, saying more than he had said in a long time. During a moment of confidence, he ordered an ugly-looking cigar from the waitress. The cigar was the first he had ever smoked. He looked toward Brownie, interested. Music played. Chrome glittered. Glass splintered. Life would go on. Jack would go with it. He was gone.